I0549350

Also by Leone Sperling

Coins for the Ferryman

Mother's Day

What about love?

Jamie

Book of Life

'Wanted – A man in his forties; good-humoured, tolerant, affectionate, sensual, intelligent.'

When Sophie meets John she enters his strange closed world. With him she finds eroticism, comfort and escape. He is her oasis.

These three interlinked novellas explore the strands of Sophie's life and her capacity to love; the powerful love that binds her to her children, the poignant love for ageing parents, and the driving search for a loving relationship with a man.

OASIS

by Leone Sperling

© Leone Sperling 2014

Leone Sperling asserts the moral right to be identified as the author of 'Oasis'

Cover design and typeset by Green Avenue Design.

First Published in 1990 by William Heinemann Australia.

This edition published by Cilento Publishing.

ISBN: 978-0-9925601-9-5

For my children – Adam, Evan, Simon and Tamara.
And remembering Steve – letter writer, love and friend.

OASIS

BETRAYAL

It's some years now since Sophie went to Nepal. The children were quite big at the time. Certainly old enough to be left. Aaron was sixteen, Paul was fourteen and Ilana twelve years old. Sophie's oldest son, Mark, was eighteen but he was overseas at the time. He had just finished high school and he thought that if he could manage to go to Europe alone, then he might be brave enough to go to university. Sophie was sure he'd manage. After all, he'd taken the fatherly role in the family since he was twelve years old. And the others, the younger ones, were reasonably mature and self-sufficient. Besides, she left the children in Jodie's care. Jodie was the family's American-born thirty-two-year-old sister-friend. She had lived in their house from time to time and had shared their lives over many years.

Sophie had a very good reason for going trekking in Nepal. Her live-in lover of four and a half years' standing had left her – suddenly, inexplicably, unexpectedly left her. She was unhappy. She needed to do something nice for herself. She thought that if she climbed and clambered her way through the mountains, up there at the top of the world, then she might find a measure of peace, recover her independence, see herself in a better perspective.

Sophie's lover had dismantled their world. She could remember the day it happened. It was a Saturday, lunchtime. She was sitting in the dining-room, eating vegetable soup. Sophie liked making vegetable soup in the winter. She made it thick and chunky. Uncooked, really, so that you had to chew it and eat it, not just swallow it. Only on this Saturday she'd had to put her soup in the food processor and mash it until it was as soft and smooth as baby food. That was the only way that she could eat it because she'd gone the day before to visit the butcher of Park Street. Of course, he's not a real butcher. He's a peridontist. Sophie had spent two hours lying on her back in his chair while he'd sliced her gums, scoured out pockets of unmentionable pollution that had collected there over the years and then stitched the gums back together again. He'd stuck a thick piece of waxy dressing right around the crescent of her mouth, pressed hard against the back of her top teeth. It had to stay there for a week.

When Sophie looked in the mirror she could see neatly tied black stitches at gum level on each of her front teeth. The black stitches made her more aware of the scattered grey hairs and the lines etched on her face. They were the lines of laughter and despair, like the Greek masks of tragedy and comedy. Once she could flash from one to the other. Now she was held in a mask of ambivalence, frozen in a face condemned to the constant revelation of opposites. Pain and joy together. A forty-five-year-old face.

So she was sitting at the dining-room table, eating her puréed vegetable soup, when she thought she heard someone calling out her name. The table was piled high with school-books, pieces of paper, pairs of socks and the usual assortment of children's possessions. She'd cleared a small space at the top end of the table so she could eat her soup there. She was wearing a pink, round-the-house track suit. It was late April. The weather was quite chilly. Her mouth was still painful and she had to concentrate hard in order to be able to swallow the soup.

She heard the voice again, 'Sophie! Sophie!' it called. The voice was twisted, harsh, distraught. It did not sound like the voice of anyone she knew. She thought she must have imagined it. She tried another mouthful of soup. 'Sophie! Come here!'

The voice was real. It came from her bedroom. It must be Michael. He'd left early that morning to go and work on his boat. He must have decided to come back home. Perhaps something was wrong.

Sophie walked down the hall and into her bedroom. He was sitting on the bed, hunched up, like Rodin's Thinker. The room was a mess. The bed was unmade and there were clothes all over the floor. Michael's large wicker laundry basket was right next to him. Although he'd lived with her for four and a half years, he still kept his clothes in a movable laundry basket. She could see that it was squashed full of his possessions.

'What's the matter?' Sophie asked. She went to him and put her hand on his shoulder. Her mouth hurt and she didn't feel like being sympathetic. Besides, he'd been a real shit over the last few weeks. He'd taken on two building jobs at the same time and he seemed to be working day and night to meet his deadlines. He'd kept her awake the night before, tossing and turning, grinding his teeth.

He turned away from her touch. He arranged himself so that his knees were tightly together, his elbows were on his knees and his chin rested on both clenched fists. He stared in the direction of the doorway. He did not look at Sophie.

'Look, I'm moving out for a while,' he said. 'I couldn't sleep at all last night. I can't go without sleep. I've got to get myself sorted out.'

She touched the top of his head, gently. 'You're just working too hard, that's all. You'll be alright as soon as you get these two jobs out of the way.'

'No, it's more than that. I've been unfaithful to you.'

Sophie took her hand away from the top of his head. She felt a sharp clutch of panic. The kind that starts in the bottom of your stomach. Empty. Cold. Her heart stopped still.

She laughed. 'This is some kind of joke, isn't it?' Michael unfaithful? Impossible!

'I'm a shit,' he cried. 'I can't live with myself. I can't live with my guilt. I can't live with you.'

'Look, we can sort this out, you know,' said Sophie, forcing his knees apart, bending down on the floor in front of him, taking his face between her hands, forcing his eyes to meet hers.

He couldn't look at her. 'All men are shits,' he declared. He'd always said that. It was a favourite expression. Until now, Sophie had thought he meant all men except himself.

'How could I do this to you?' he asked. It was no good asking Sophie. She didn't know the answer. He was the only man in whom she had ever placed an absolute trust. 'These four years have been the happiest years of my life. I've never loved anyone as much as I've loved you. No one has ever known me the way you do.'

Sophie moved away from him. 'Who is she?'

'No one you know.'

'Is it serious?'

'No. I just need to sort myself out.'

Sophie felt quite calm, just for a moment. 'It's over, isn't it. You're never coming back.'

He brushed away a few tears. 'Don't say that. Don't make me burn my bridges.' What was he crying for? He was the one who had been unfaithful. He was the one who was leaving. His tears infuriated her.

'What about the future?' she cried. 'What about the boat? We were going to sail around the world in your bloody boat and live happily ever after. What about me? What's going to happen to me?'

He couldn't handle that. 'I'm going to stay at my mother's for a while,' he said, picking up his laundry basket. 'I want to give you back this cassette player.'

'I don't want it back,' she screamed. Sophie had only given it to him the week before. It was a nice radio-cassette. She'd given it to him as an early birthday present, to cheer him up because he seemed to be depressed.

'Living here was like being in a huge, warm womb,' he said. Then he picked up his things and went out. He didn't say good-bye to any of the kids. He was too embarrassed. And he didn't say what he was going to do about all the possessions he had stored in her garage, a massive boat engine, two tall aluminium masts, an assortment of old furniture and paintings, together with a large collection of geological books and specimens. She could hear his old Kombi van struggling to a noisy start and she listened to it rattling its way down the street.

Then Sophie went out into the lounge-room. The kids were all there, sitting in the velvet beanbags, watching TV. Jodie was with them. She was living with the family at the time.

'Michael's left me,' Sophie said. They all gathered around her asking questions. 'What?' 'Who?' 'Why?' Sophie had no answers. They were all shocked. Numbed by disbelief. Jodie hugged Sophie and got out the Tarot cards. 'Come on, Sophie, I'll do a reading.' Jodie made Sophie shuffle the cards and then she laid them out, slowly, calmly. The card that dominated the reading was a picture of a sword piercing a bleeding heart.

And that is just how Sophie felt, as if her heart had been torn into pieces. She went into her bedroom and lay down on the bed. The situation was so intolerable that she stepped outside of herself, momentarily, and looked at her disintegrated parts. She tried to find there some remnant of the wholesome, independent person she had been before Michael came to live with her.

When Sophie first met Michael she considered herself to be a liberated woman. She had been married and divorced. She had been a single parent for four years. She had been through the sexual revolution. She knew what she wanted from a man. She wanted a comfortable, committed, part-time relationship with a warm, affectionate, tolerant, good-humoured human being. She knew her limitations. She knew she couldn't live with a man, not after the years of struggle, not after the effort to know herself, not after the battle for independence. She loved her kids, fiercely, like a lioness. She guarded their close, tight bonds. No, living with a man was absolutely out of the question. And she didn't want anyone else's shit. Above all else, she didn't want any man to lay his shit on her ever again. She was finished with all of that.

She saw her path clearly. All the gnarled roots and dense bush and tangled undergrowth had been hacked away. All she and her kids had to do was to keep travelling, straight ahead. Those kids were her best friends. She knew that. They were life's greatest challenge; it's greatest reward.

The trouble was that the kids were not enough. She often wanted to lie in some man's arms and feel the fur on his chest and tuck her head into the curve of his neck and rest there.

When Sophie met Michael she felt very sure of herself and very satisfied with her development as a human being. Although she wanted to find a suitable lover, she felt quite capable of going on alone. She'd made plenty of mistakes in her involvements with men over the last five years and she didn't intend to make any more. She was only interested in a man who could accept the way she and her kids had to live their lives.

Sophie had stopped believing in nuclear families and she certainly didn't want another father for her children. Since her marriage had ended, her large house had become something of an experiment in communal living. Sophie found that the children responded very well to having another adult living in the house who was neither a father nor a mother. She certainly needed someone else to help her with the children and the college where Sophie taught was a good source for providing mature students who were looking for accommodation in return for baby-sitting.

The first of these students was Jodie. Actually, Jodie had come to live at the house a few months before Sophie's marriage ended. It was a difficult time for Sophie. She needed someone else in the house to provide stability for the children while she and her husband battled their way to the conclusion of their shredded marriage. She asked her class if any of them were interested in a live-in baby-sitting job.

Jodie came out after class. She told Sophie that she had been living with her boyfriend but that the relationship was not working. She said that she had left him; that she had nowhere to live; that she had very little money; that she missed her own family, who lived in America; that she loved children; that she longed for a surrogate family to live with and share with and belong to.

Jodie looked like a peaceful person. She always wore Indian clothes. She never used make-up. Her long, lank hair was absolutely straight. It was browny-blonde, mouse-coloured. Her fingers and toes were long, thin, white. She liked to wear rings on her thumbs. She wore traditional, genuine, flat-heeled Indian leather sandals. She smelled of sandalwood and her clothes carried the aroma of incense. She wore large rose-coloured glasses. Her movements were slow, unhurried.

Sophie took her home. They all fell in love with her. Ilana was three years old, then. Paul was five, Aaron seven and Mark nine. Jodie made it her business to understand the individual nature of each child. She was very patient and very calm. She spent time with the children; playing, talking, stroking, loving. She instinctively knew when an argument was imminent and had the uncanny knack of defusing an explosive outburst before it began. With her slow, quiet drawl, she entranced the children with stories of her childhood in America and London. She recited funny poems and related intriguing stories of strange encounters. She fed their fantasies and soothed their fears and anxieties. She was twenty-four years old.

Jodie became Sophie's best friend. She comforted Sophie and gave her the courage to survive the last rending months of the marriage. 'You'll be alright, Sophie,' she would say. 'You're strong and you've got these wonderful kids. You don't know how lucky you are. I'd give anything to have kids like yours.'

It always seemed to Sophie that Jodie was older and wiser than herself. She would talk to Sophie of her harsh adolescence, of a need to rebel against parental control, of exposure to a world of men and sex and drugs and abortions, of being old at fourteen. Jodie had lived through a sordid world that was alien to Sophie's gentle, Jewish, middle-class background. She had survived her nightmare journey and come through it – whole, pure, integrated, calm, complete. Or so it seemed to Sophie.

After the marriage came to an end, Jodie and the kids and Sophie had a joyous time. It was the Christmas school holidays. They would go to the drive-in in Jodie's old Holden station wagon and the kids used to lie on a mattress on the roof to watch the movie. They would go to the beach during the day and eat hamburgers and French-fries and chocolate and caramel sundaes at McDonald's. They would lie in the velvet beanbags and watch movies on the television. They never did any housework. Decadence, of a kind.

'I really love you, Sophie,' Jodie would say, 'and I really love the kids.' And she meant it and they felt it and whatever she gave them, they gave back to her so the house was a circle of love and warmth and the idea of any man having ever lived there seemed to fade away. A great dark cloud had lifted from their lives and they spun themselves in gentle, airy threads of love. It was both satisfying and sufficient but only while the children were there. Two nights a week the children would stay with their father and when they were away Sophie did not want to be with Jodie. When the children were away, Sophie wanted men and sex, excitement and lust. And then, when they came back, she longed to slide once more into the golden innocence of Jodie and the children and the consuming bonds of mothering.

After five or six months, Jodie decided to live with her boyfriend again. Not alone. In a shared house, at Crows Nest. The house was full of vegetarians who were doing courses in therapeutic massage. Jodie often came to Sophie's house and Sophie and the children often went to hers. Jodie took the children out frequently, either singly or en masse. She had nearly completed a six-month course in massage. She often practiced on the children but Sophie would never allow Jodie to practise on her. She felt uncomfortable about being touched by Jodie in that way.

When Jodie left, a student called Sally took over. She was a brash girl, with big breasts and long, straight, red hair. She smoked a great deal and it soon became clear that her ideas on how children should behave were very different from Sophie's. Before Sophie knew what was happening she'd moved in a double bed and a boyfriend. Sophie put up with this for a few months and then told Sally she would have to go.

At that time there was a young man from Portugal in Sophie's English class. His name was Joseph. He was small and slim, dark-haired, with a brown skin and flecked hazel eyes. Sophie had become Joseph's friend because she was still an idealistic teacher who believed in doing more than the job required. She made a real effort to get to know her students, to look for problems, to offer assistance. Joseph's English was very good and he showed a natural flair in his study of English literature, but he obviously needed extra help in grammar and sentence structure. In the process of helping Joseph with his English, Sophie found that what Joseph really needed was an opportunity to talk to someone about his family.

He told Sophie of a childhood so traumatic that she wondered how he had survived it at all. Until he was fourteen, Joseph had lived with his mother and father in Portugal. His father had been withdrawn, insane, violent. His mother refused to share a bed with her husband. Instead she took Joseph into her bed as a protection and as a comfort. When Joseph was fourteen years old, she suddenly took him and ran off with another man. She divorced her husband and married her lover. They had come to Australia two years ago and the marriage had been cemented by the birth of Joseph's baby sister.

Joseph told this story many times. He was like the Ancient Mariner. The telling provided only momentary respite. It did not cure him. Sophie tried to help him analyse his feelings, his resentment towards the stepfather for taking his mother away from the bed she had willingly shared with her son for so many years. There were many arguments in his house, caused by the conflict his mother faced, torn as she was between the fused, clinging bond that the past had created with Joseph and the demands of a new husband and baby. He hated living there but was afraid to leave.

When Sophie decided that Sally was unsuitable as a baby-sitter, she talked to Joseph. She persuaded him to leave home and live with her and the children. She told him that such a step would provide him with a good half-way house. He would be independent of his family, but he would not have to fend for himself. She would provide him with a room and food in return for baby-sitting, gardening and taking the rubbish to the tip. Soon he would be going to university and his living allowance would provide him with pocket money. It would be a good arrangement for them both. Joseph agreed. He was Sophie's permanent, reliable, live-in babysitter for just over three years.

The wonderful thing about Joseph was that he was unobtrusive. He was so quiet in his habits and so soft in his speech that he seemed to blend into the background of the house. Except for her son Paul, Sophie and her children were all rather loud – raucous, prone to emotional outbursts, shouting matches, vigorous tears. They could not have lived with anyone else who was as irrepressible or as vocal as they were. Perhaps that's why they attracted quiet people – like Jodie and Joseph. Perhaps such people obtained some vicarious pleasure from the vitality of Sophie's household.

Sophie used to have a housekeeper come to clean the house once a week. The night before she came, the family would have to pick up all the toys and clothes and possessions that had somehow become scattered all over the floors. Invariably, this would coincide with a night that Sophie had to teach. She would say to Joseph, 'Please make the kids clean up the place tonight.'

'Only if I can do it without shouting at them,' he would reply. He was never angry with any child. Although he didn't cook, he washed up the dishes every night and he did everything he could to help Sophie.

He didn't go out with girls. His male friends came to visit him. They would go into his room, talk, listen to music. They did all these things very quietly. Nothing about Joseph disturbed Sophie.

Joseph was an adult companion. Often he and Sophie would go to the movies or to the theatre while the children were at their father's. He never expected to go out with her but if she asked him he never refused.

He watched her. He witnessed her mistakes. He saw her blunder her way through one disastrous sexual relationship after another and never commented, never judged, never disapproved.

There was a physical taboo between them. She never touched him. If he passed her in the hallway, he would step aside, press himself against the wall, so that no physical contact could possibly occur. Sometimes he would pick a single rose from the garden and place it in a small vase next to her bed.

She knew that he toyed with homosexuality but he did not practise it in her house. Perhaps he did not practise it at all. It was not something that they talked about.

She knew that he slept with a girl one night at her house and she was pleased, but nothing came of it and she had to watch him drift closer and closer towards making the alternative choice. She thought that, in some way, he wanted her to save him but she could not have taken that step. Sometimes you can look into the eyes of another human being and know, instantly, that to be drawn into that person's world would mean inevitable tragedy. One can read one's death in another's eyes. That's how she felt about Joseph. There was a love of a kind between them but she would not have dared to plunge into it. She knew too much about Oedipus.

The thing she appreciated most about Joseph was that he understood the way she had chosen to live with her children. He did not try to change anything and she interpreted this as approval. He accepted the rules of the house. He understood that beneath the untidiness, the chaos and the appearance of children doing exactly as they pleased, there lay a complex web of unstated laws that everyone in the household obeyed.

Joseph lived with them until he finished his university studies. By then Sophie knew that he was committed to homosexuality and he left them to go overseas to pursue a love relationship. His going was an easy parting. Sophie no longer needed a live-in baby-sitter and he no longer needed Sophie.

Sophie and the children had been living alone for a about a year when she met Michael. Both she and the children had come to see the family as an amorphous unit that could expand or contract to accommodate the needs of the moment. Jodie and Joseph were part of that family and the children's friends could move in and out of the house with very little disruption. It is true that Sophie wanted to find a man who would be her friend and lover forever, but she certainly didn't want anyone who would interfere with the way she ran her household.

When Sophie first saw Michael she liked him because his shirt was hanging out, his beard was bit untidy and his hair had been cut so badly that it stuck out in tufts. Sophie liked men who looked like that. His nose was large and his eyes soft and gentle. She managed to find out, fairly quickly, that he was thirty-nine, divorced, had two children whom he saw once a week, worked as a carpenter, used to be a geologist and that he was building a forty-two foot steel boat.

He managed to find out that she was forty-one, divorced, had four children who lived with her constantly, was a teacher and that she had written a novel, that, so far, no one wanted to publish.

Sophie hated going to parties but she was glad she'd gone to this one. By the end of the evening she had learned that he lived in a communal household, was an armchair communist, approved of homosexuals and didn't aspire to being anyone's husband or father.

The first time they went out together he took her to a five o'clock movie. They saw Newsfront. During the movie he sat so that his shoulder touched hers but he didn't try to hold her hand. After the movie, while they were walking to the restaurant, he took her hand, awkwardly, and held it as they ambled down the street. They ate at The Eastern in Dixon Street. He ordered king prawns in hoi sin sauce. It was the first time she's ever tasted hoi sin sauce. While they ate he talked almost exclusively about the last relationship he'd been involved in. It seemed to have been a pretty violent one. He looked so mild and gentle that she couldn't imagine what had attracted him to a woman who actually used to beat him up. She talked about the last relationship she had been involved in. It had been a destructive one, and in this airing of the past they cleared the space between them, as divorced people often do. Afterwards they walked along Balmoral Beach and then they went back to her place and went to bed. They came together not with lust, nor with passionate intensity. Rather, they joined each other with a sense of relief, a feeling of harmony and peace, a gentle caring that could easily go on forever and ever. Despite all their experiences to the contrary, Sophie and Michael both believed in forever.

When she first invited him to dinner, the children behaved obnoxiously. They undid his shoelaces and tied them to the chair he was sitting on. Every second word they uttered was 'fuck' or 'cunt' or 'shit'. They dominated the conversation. The boys put on what looked like a life-threatening wrestling match and Sophie's seven-year-old daughter kept saying things like, 'I suppose you think you can come here and tell us what to do.'

Michael kept smiling, tolerantly. Sophie tried to maintain order by being calm and rational. She tried to bring up conversations that would interest the children and show Michael that they were not just aggressive little monsters but intelligent and individualistic human beings. 'God,' and 'communism' were always good topics for that. At 9.30 pm it was bedtime. The boys rough and tumbled loudly down the stairs to their rooms and her daughter's parting comment to Michael, was 'And when are you moving in?' All this behaviour simply meant that the children liked Michael and that he had passed their test.

In Sophie's bedroom, after the children had already gone to sleep, Michael told her that he would be ready to sail his boat around the world in four or five years' time. Sophie must have looked forlorn. Here she was, a lady with four kids ranging in age from seven to thirteen and he was telling her that he was going to go off and sail around the world.

'I can wait, you know,' he said, 'until the kids are old enough for you to leave them. I'll build a walnut writing desk for you, in the aft cabin.' She wept in his arms. 'I think everyone needs a soul mate,' he said, stroking her hair clumsily, consoling her. 'Someone you can share everything with. Someone you sleep with every night. Someone you go everywhere with. Don't you?'

This is what Sophie wanted to say: she wanted to say, 'Now look here, I'm an independent woman. I like sleeping alone. I don't want to be anyone's soul mate. I want to be myself.' But she didn't say those words. She couldn't say them because the truth of the matter was that the years had been hard and lonely and here was this man who wanted to fill in all her spaces and the longing to be cushioned and held and adored and worshipped; the need to have every corner of her being filled to overflowing with some man's love was so attractive that he seduced and won her in an instant.

'Yes,' Sophie replied. 'Yes, everyone needs a soul mate, yes, yes, yes.' And so, with willing acquiescence it all began – their coupling, their mating, their 'marriage'.

Michael couldn't believe his luck. He'd found a woman who didn't want him to mow lawns or cook barbecues on Sundays, someone who understood that he had to build the boat and that meant working at it every weekend.

Sophie couldn't believe her luck. She's found a man who didn't expect her to entertain him on Saturdays and Sundays. She could spend the time with her kids or get on with her writing.

He told her she looked like a Russian princess. He thought their love was as great as the love of Antony and Cleopatra. He declared his love endlessly and, although Sophie answered, 'I love you too', the words had to be conjured up and they came somewhat unwillingly out of her mouth. What Sophie felt was warmth. She felt comfort. She felt security. She felt certainty. Sophie did not need to rush into his arms the moment he entered the door. She felt no great bounding rush of sexual desire. Sophie was too busy; teaching full-time, looking after the kids, cooking, washing, ironing, writing.

'You're my only friend,' Michael would tell her. It was true. Sophie noticed that, although he had a few acquaintances who invited him to the occasional party, he did not appear to have any close friends.

'I never learned how to communicate with women,' he complained. That didn't surprise Sophie. After all, he'd been bundled off to boarding school at such an early age that he'd never had a chance to get to know his mother or his sister.

'And I can't be really close to my kids – I don't see them often enough.' Sophie found it very easy to become all that he needed her to be.

At least once a week, for four and a half years, he would say to her: 'You'll never leave me, will you? If you left me I'd kill myself. If you left me I'd go down to the boat and smash great holes in it.'

No wonder she felt secure. Sophie smiled when she heard his kombi van arriving home. She had learned a very important thing. She never wanted to be lonely, ever again.

It was not really a marriage because he had no concept of sharing. He never interfered in what went on between Sophie and her children and for that she was grateful. But he never helped. Sometimes he washed up the dishes. He would go into her bedroom at night and watch the television there. He wanted Sophie to go in there with him but domestic tasks usually occupied her until after eight o'clock. Perhaps the children needed help with their homework. She didn't want to watch television. She was used to climbing into bed at the end of the day and reading a book. She couldn't read with the television on. She learned to compromise and adjust.

He worked so hard physically – five days a week at being a carpenter, two days a week on the boat. The only days he ever took off were her birthday and Christmas day. He used to get so tired that the few beers or the wine he had with his dinner would send him off to sleep. Sophie often found herself sitting up next to a snoring man watching the end of a television program that she didn't want to see in the first place.

Michael was mean about money because every cent had to go into building this boat of his, but he was not mean about birthdays and he was not mean about Friday nights. Every Friday night he would take Sophie out to a restaurant and to see a film or a play. She knew more about films and plays than he did and he preferred her to make all the decisions about where they would go. Every birthday and Christmas he would give her something beautiful – a piece of jewellery that he would take her to select.

Although Michael was not an intellectual, he wanted to learn and he wanted Sophie to teach him how to expand his mind. He loved it when Sophie gave him lists of books to read. He found it difficult to explain why he liked or disliked particular books but he expected Sophie to analyse them for him. He especially liked it when Sophie explained to him the underlying meaning of a film or play. He did not want to contribute to these discussions. He only wanted to listen to her.

Six months after they began living together, Sophie's novel was accepted for publication. Michael was terribly proud of her and told everyone he met or worked for that his lady was a writer. Sophie felt comfortable being with a man who took pride in her achievements, instead of envying them.

What Sophie appreciated about Michael were his practical qualities. She admired the fanatical dedication with which he approached the building of his boat. It was his life's work. It obsessed him. He liked to make love, slowly and gently, but she knew that the moment he'd had his orgasm his thoughts would go back to the boat. They snuggled together all night, curled into each other, glued up like jelly babies. Michael made life bearable for Sophie, securing her against the practical difficulties of life – of working, mothering, writing.

Michael was a child and he joined her sons in childish pranks, often provoking them to more outrageous behaviour. Sophie often felt she had five children instead of four, but she liked that quality in him. He tried to make life fun. And he liked to show the boys how to do practical things. Mark went down to the boat with him every Saturday, helping to put the heavy steel plates onto the boat's frame. He even took Aaron with him sometimes and told Sophie that Aaron took to welding as if he's been born to it. He like Paul's soft and gentle nature and found his absentmindedness amusing. He thought Ilana was delightfully outrageous and insisted that she had taught him swearwords that he'd never heard before.

'I wish we could have a baby,' Michael would say.

'Who'd look after it?' Sophie would ask.

'I would,' he'd reply. 'I'd take it to work with me and put it in a playpen. I'd give it a hammer to play with.'

'If I were pregnant, I'd have an abortion,' Sophie would say. 'I'd get the foetus and put it in a plastic bag and throw it away in the rubbish bin.'

Michael irritated Sophie sometimes, but the warmth and comfort outweighed the irritation. Sophie had stopped being an independent woman. Sophie had become a wife. Michael had grown to be a part of her, like one of her fingers or toes.

At first Sophie did not know what to do when Michael left her. She couldn't eat. She couldn't sleep. She thought he might be going through some mid-life crisis and in some ways she even felt sorry for him. She spent her time with the kids and Jodie, watching commercial television shows, hugging everyone, cuddling. She cried in bed at night. She couldn't watch the news on the ABC because she knew he would be watching it. She couldn't read the Letters to the Editor in the Sydney Morning Herald because she knew he read them every morning.

After five days she felt so worried about Michael that she rang up his mother to ask her to be kind to him. His mother said that she hadn't seen him at all. When Sophie heard that, she knew that Michael had been lying to her. He wasn't just 'sorting himself out'. She knew that he would never come back.

The sensible part of Sophie realised that she had to get on with things. She had to get back to being herself. She told herself, very firmly, that she was not shattered; she was not destroyed; she was just disjointed, out of harmony with herself. There was an empty space beside her and she had to find some way to overcome that loss. The best thing would be to plan a holiday for herself. If she could get away alone then she would be able to pull herself together, she would be able to find herself again, she would be able to prepare herself for whatever life might have in store for her. Sophie talked the matter over with Jodie and Jodie said yes, she'd be happy to stay with the kids and look after them and take Sophie's place for a while. The next day Sophie went into town and booked to go trekking in Nepal. She was due to leave the day after Christmas.

There was, however, a darker side to Sophie, a part of herself that was more devastated than she cared to admit. Sophie blamed herself for Michael's departure. She thought she had not loved him enough. She thought she had taken him too much for granted. She thought that, in some subtle and unconscious way, she and the kids had pushed him out. She thought she had put the kids first and that's why he had left. She would never close her bedroom door while they made love. She always had to have part of herself listening for the children. Often she couldn't be bothered about making love at all. No wonder he'd gone off and found someone else.

Self-castigation gave way to mountainous rage when she found out that he had not been staying at his mother's place. She was consumed with a fury so great that she wanted to kill him. She wrote him horrible, twisted letters, full of hate and bitterness and posted them to his mother's address. She wished he were impotent. She wished he were dead.

She decided to confront him. She rang the boatyard, found out his phone number, rang up and demanded to speak to him. It was a Thursday evening. Seven p.m.

'I have to see you,' she said.

'When?'

'Now,' she replied. 'I'll meet you in half an hour, in Willoughby Road, outside the Vietnamese restaurant.

He was there when she arrived. He got into her car. 'I want to know where I stand,' she said. 'I've spent five days feeling sorry for you when I could have spent them thinking what a shit you are.'

'I've been living with this lady,' he said, quite meekly. 'I think I love her but that doesn't mean I love you any the less. She wants to have my baby.'

Sophie felt swift stabs of confused emotions – hatred, jealousy, fear and guilt at her own persistent refusal to even consider having Michael's child. She did not allow these feeling to show. All she let him see was her anger.

'You shit,' said Sophie. 'You don't know the first thing about love!'

'I think it's quite possible to love two people at the same time, don't you?'

'What's the good of loving me if you live with her? What about loyalty? What about fidelity? What about all those things we agreed about? How could you have betrayed me? I would never have betrayed you. And how could you let me think you were just sorting yourself out?' She turned on the ignition, crunched into first gear, revved the car into the line of city-bound traffic and sped off down the highway.

'Where are you going?' cried Michael. 'Stop the car!'

'We're going to Kings Cross for a cup of coffee,' she replied.

'I can't go with you!' he cried, alarmed. 'Let me out!'

'You'll do exactly what I say,' Sophie insisted.

'You're so hard!' he cried, holding onto the seat of the car.

'It's shits like you who've made me hard! And what's more, I know who you're living with. It's that woman you did a job for a year or so ago, the one who had a copy of my novel on her coffee table, the one who wants to be a writer. She was all excited about you because you actually lived with me. She wanted to meet me, didn't she? She wanted me to look at her writing. That's who it is, isn't it!'

'How did you find out?' he asked, anguished.

'I'm clever, that's all. You told me you'd run into her again. What is she? Some kind of spider, some kind of twentieth-century Lorelei, some predatory creature from outer space? Who the hell does she think she is? You don't belong to her, you belong to me!'

Michael kept quiet. He held on tight and hoped Sophie wouldn't smash up the car.

'For Heaven's sake! All I want is a cup of coffee,' Sophie cried. Of course, Sophie wanted much more than a cup of coffee. She wanted to be thirty-five instead of forty-five. She wanted love and marriage and Michael. She wanted to be the new lover he had just acquired. Not the old one he was discarding.

Michael got out of the car. 'Calm down a bit,' he pleaded. 'Let me hold your hand while we're walking down the street.' Sophie laughed. She could tell he was afraid of her and his fear sent power coursing through her, head to toe. She took his hand and they walked down the street, quite jauntily, like lovers.

They went into a coffee shop and he ordered a Cappuccino for himself and a Vienna coffee for Sophie. They didn't talk. They watched the people passing by. She felt cool and calm. When they had finished their coffee, she drove him back to Willoughby Road.

'I don't know what to say to you,' he said, as he opened the car door to get out.

Sophie burst into tears. 'You don't belong to her. You're a part of me,' Sophie wailed.

Michael tried to touch her. 'Everything will be alright,' he said, but she pushed his hand away.

'What disgusts me most about myself,' she said, 'is that I would actually take you back.' Then she hit him, hard across the face. 'Get out,' she screamed, 'get out of my car!'

'Will you be alright?' he asked.

'No,' she creamed, 'No!' and drove off, weeping with rage.

He rang the next day to make sure she was still alive. 'You'd better come and get your things out of the garage,' she said coldly, 'and if any more mail arrives here for you, I'm gong to throw it straight into the rubbish bin.'

'Won't you send it on to me?' he begged. 'You could just send it to my mother's.'

'No, you should have told the post office your change of address.'

'I can't move the boat engine yet.'

'You've got one week to get that engine out of my garage,' Sophie warned. 'If it's not gone by next Friday I'm going to pour sand and honey into it.'

'Won't you give me a bit longer? I'll have to get a truck with a crane. It'll be expensive and I'm a bit short of money right now.'

'I wouldn't wait any longer than next Friday if I were you,' replied Sophie.

He came for his things and for his engine within a week. 'I can't look at you,' Michael said to her. But Sophie could look at him. She looked at him coldly, with hate. She wanted to get an axe and chop off his prick and slice off his balls.

Sophie was immobilized with anger. She couldn't go out for six months; she couldn't go to a film or a play; she couldn't eat at a restaurant and she couldn't touch a man.

After six months Sophie decided that celibacy was a bit dangerous and she took steps to find another lover. The man she came across was not a bit like Michael. He wasn't looking for a life-time mate. He was looking for regular sexual encounters without love. He didn't want to take her out for dinner. He didn't want to go with her to see films or plays. He didn't want to meet the children. Although this situation seemed strange to Sophie at first, she found that arrangement suited her very well for the time being. Sophie was ready for sex but she was not ready to take the risk of loving again.

Two weeks before she left for Nepal, she got the following letter from Michael.

Dear Sophie,

I think this is the first letter I've ever written to you. You may not read this any further. I have no idea what your feelings are to me now, but I have sadness at present – over the last few months, wondering how you are. I have caught the merest glimpse of you one or two times.

At such times I feel a mixture of embarrassment, shame, sorrow and regret all in small doses which I rationalize and then suppress.

Anyway, how are you? I am waiting for your next book. I check at the bookshops regularly.

How are the kids?

I'm not going to write any more because it may be in vain. I have a feeling I could write twenty pages comfortably.

Warm wishes and a big hug if it is accepted.

Michael

If Michael's letter was a tentative holding out of the hand, then Sophie had at last had her revenge. She took out her metaphorical axe and chopped off his fingers, one by one. She wrote him a letter in which she said that she had a new lover, that she was perfectly happy, that she was really glad to be rid of Michael, and that the thing she wanted most from life was never, never to hear from or see him ever again.

Sophie was determined to stop thinking about Michael and she tried to concentrate on Nepal. She had chosen Nepal because it provided her with a physical challenge. Would she, at forty-five, be capable of enduring a trek through the Himalayas? She certainly believed so and she jogged a mile every morning and ran up and down their steep staircase at least twenty times a day to prepare herself for what she considered to be an adventurous undertaking. However, there was another reason for choosing Nepal. People she knew, who had been there, spoke of the spiritual aspects of such a journey. Would she, through the constant necessity of having to put one foot in front of the other, be able to transcend her habitual day-to-day concern for self? Would the Himalayas be able to transform her from a total pragmatist into a spiritual being? She thought that a change of that magnitude would be most unlikely but a small part of her yearned for just such a transformation.

To Sophie the world seemed harsh and cruel and real. There was only life and death. She was not the reincarnation of anything. This was her first life, her only life, and when she died she would rot in the ground. Maggots would eat her flesh. She'd asked the children to throw copies of her books into her grave. The measure of her meaning. Her beautiful daughter, Ilana, had suggested putting some symbol of herself into the grave – an egg whisk, she thought, to remind Sophie of her child's career as a world-famous chef. Sophie supposed the boys would make a contribution too. Paul, her tender songwriter-poet-musician would no doubt thrust a specially composed poem into the earth with her, and Aaron, the dashing dark-eyed film maker would certainly find a celluloid offering to leave with her. What about Mark, though? Solid, responsible Mark was not a creator. He was a fixer. A laterally thinking fixer, moreover. He could fix toilets, bathroom heaters, clothes driers, garage doors, vacuum cleaners, clocks, electric cords, car stereos and light fittings. Perhaps he'd bury a screw-driver with her, or a hammer.

Sophie could imagine her funeral. She could picture the rabbi's face, his scowl of disapproval at the sight of the bundle of precious objects her children would insist must accompany her. What was wrong with burial offerings? The Egyptians did it. The children would smile. They would enjoy being slightly outrageous. Their gesture would unite them as they had always been united; the children and Sophie, welded together against the harshness of the world. Once Sophie had written an article for a newspaper about the Palm Sunday Anti-Nuclear march. The photographer had wanted to capture the family on camera, walking hand in hand through the lounge-room. He would have used the garden, he said, but on the day he came to photograph them it was pouring with rain. They all fell about at the thought of actually being seen hand in hand. Their bonds were not of that visible kind.

Being such a pragmatist, Sophie was attracted to the spirituality of others. Life would be so much easier if she could believe in something beyond the starkness of reality.

That was one of the things Sophie found attractive about Jodie when she first came to live in their house. Jodie was a spiritual person. She believed in yoga, tai chi, Tarot cards, meditation, astrology, reincarnation and herbal remedies. When Jodie moved into the shared house at Crows Nest, Sophie envied her. Sophie's own passions, anxieties, lusts and minor neuroses seemed magnified out of all proportion when she surveyed the calm and tranquil setting of Jodie's life style.

Of course, Sophie could see that Jodie's life stood still. She could see that reading Tarot cards and doing yoga and being paid for the occasional massage did not add up to a worthwhile existence. Sophie realized that, in contrast to Jodie's life, her own propulsion through day-to-day problems did amount to something. The demands of single parenting, swinging from elation to despair; the difficulties of teaching, preparation and marking; the pain of not being able to write, the joy of some-times being able to write; all these were positive expressions of some vital life force. They added up to success and achieve-ment of a kind. Despite exhaustion, Sophie plunged through her working days like an engine revved to full capacity. And yet she looked at Jodie and longed to be like her. Jodie was so cool, so easy, so still. Washing her hair could be regarded as sufficient activity for a whole day. Sitting in the garden in a lotus position, eyes closed, meditating, her hair drying in the sun. How Sophie wished she could be like that.

Sophie continued to watch Jodie's life and continued to admire it. She was pleased when Jodie decided to go back to America to face her own family, to live with them again and to work through any problems she might have with them. While she was in America, Jodie completed a course which qualified her to work with retarded adolescents.

Sophie and the children missed her but they wrote to each other all the time. Jodie was homesick for Australia. Her letters were full of longing. She was still their sister; despite her absence, she kept her place in the family because she had carved out that place so carefully, so skillfully, so uniquely that no one else could have filled the particular space she left behind her.

Sophie used to write to Jodie whenever she was sad or depressed. She would send Jodie poems and stories she had written. Jodie would write back saying, 'I read your poetry and your stories and I re-read all the letters you've sent me. I don't claim to understand you, but I know you'd never lie to me. You can make me think, which sometimes hurts but is never undesirable. So please write and tell me you've cheered up! You are so beautiful when you smile. I still remember the first time I ever saw you with your shining eyes and quizzical smile. I hope I never stop knowing you.'

Her letters to the children revealed her extraordinary capacity for knowing what each child would like to hear. There were humorous drawings, interesting anecdotes, exciting, forgotten thoughts scribbled in the margins. Ilana missed her the most. She could talk to Jodie for hours, about life, relationships, growing up, the ways of the world – a sister ally against the male onslaught of three large brothers.

She came back to Australia through Africa and India. She wanted to study baby massage in Madras. The family received letters from all kinds of exotic and fascinating places. She was due back in November. They weren't sure of the exact date.

One morning Sophie got a phone call from British Airways asking her to come to the airport to pick Jodie up. She knew something must be wrong. When Sophie saw Jodie she was shocked. Her eyes were huge and her face hollowed. Her skin was yellow and her body so thin that she looked like a concentration camp survivor.

'Oh, Sophie,' she cried, 'I've been so ill. I've had hepatitis. I knew you'd look after me, if only I could get back to you.' She'd been sick for seven weeks.

Sophie took her home and put her to bed. Aaron gave up his room for her and he shared with Paul. She lived with them for a year. It took at least six months of that time for her to get well. When Michael left, Jodie jokingly suggested that it had been her fault. Perhaps she was a jinx. Wasn't it a coincidence that she was living in the house at the time of the marriage break-up and now when Michael had left? Sophie did not find it strange. She found it fortuitous. Jodie's presence was comforting and reassuring. Jodie lived with the family until a month before Sophie left for Nepal. She moved into a flat at Manly but she would come back to the house to look after the children while Sophie was away.

A few months before Sophie left for Nepal, she received a letter from Joseph saying that he would be returning to Australia shortly and hoped to see the family.

Unlike Jodie, Joseph had not maintained close contact and Sophie had very little knowledge of his life overseas. He wrote to her occasionally and she knew he had taught English in Italy for a few years. He'd been to Paris and had visited his mother and young sister who had left Australia and were living in Portugal. He never wrote to the children. Nevertheless, Sophie and the children and Jodie were all pleased to hear that he was coming back. Sophie assumed that his love relationship had come to an end. When he arrived back, he told her that he had spent the past few months with his mother in a state of terrible illness. He thought he would die there. He had developed a dreadful throat condition. His throat muscles would constantly contract and close, causing extreme pain. His mother had taken him to many specialists but no one could find the cause of this ailment and he said that he felt he had to get away and come back to Australia, in the hope that he would recover if he could escape from his mother.

He was very nervous. Very disordered. Sophie told him there was no point in seeing throat specialists. 'Your problem isn't physical, Joseph,' she said. 'It's psychological. You will have to get psychiatric help. Can't you see? Your mother is strangling you.'

'But I feel it, here, the soreness in my throat.'

'Of course you feel it physically, but it's mentally induced. You can't cure it with pills. You can only cure it by understanding the problem, by working through it.'

Sophie sent him to her own doctor to get a referral to a psychiatrist but he found her doctor unsympathetic. She sent him to a holistic doctor who was kinder but didn't do him much good. Joseph was desperate. Despite his university degree and his teaching experience in Italy, he could get no work. He told Sophie that he thought he was going mad. He was staying with friends but he felt he was imposing on them, so Sophie suggested that he could use Mark's room as Mark was away on his pre-university overseas trip for the next three months. Staying with the family would give Joseph a couple of months to get himself together.

She thought she was doing the right thing. It is impossible to stay depressed for too long in Sophie's house because it is full of children and exuberance and vitality. The members of the household all get a bit depressed at times but, on the whole, the house reverberates with a joyous sense of life. The children were fond of Joseph. They thought it was a good idea that he should stay.

So Joseph moved in, at the end of November, just four weeks before Sophie was due to leave for Nepal. It only took a few days for Sophie to realize that Joseph was not just depressed. He was decidedly disturbed. When you walked past his room there was absolutely no sound. No light and no sound. No movement. Only stillness. Only deathly quiet. What was he doing in there? He did not wash. He did not eat. Sometimes he emerged and came up into the kitchen to make himself a cup of tea or coffee or to get a can of beer or a glass of whisky. He kept beer in the fridge and he always had a bottle of whisky on the kitchen bench.

Sophie wanted to help him but he wouldn't let her. He would not communicate with her. He would murmur a few words and then go down to his room again. She used to wonder how he could stay so long in his room in the mornings without going to the toilet. He might have been dead, for all they knew. He used to go out late at night, when they were all asleep. Sometimes Sophie would hear him, coming and going.

Sophie felt that she had the power to manipulate and control everything in her own little world. After observing Joseph's behaviour for a couple of weeks, Sophie decided to write him a letter. She had to resort to letter-writing because Joseph continued to keep himself out of the way whenever she was around. She told him that his behaviour was quite unacceptable, that he couldn't lock himself in his room, day after day, that he was living in a house full of children. She did that, believing absolutely that her words would have the power to change Joseph's behaviour. But Joseph was hovering on the edge of darkness and her letter made no difference. Sophie felt concerned about going away and leaving him in the house.

'Don't worry, Mum,' said Aaron. 'Everything will be alright. For heaven's sake, Joseph lived with us for three years. After you've gone, we'll sort him out.' Sophie couldn't help noticing that sixteen-year-old Aaron was taking his role as oldest male in the family very seriously now that big brother Mark was out of the way.

'Joseph's a very nice person,' chipped in Ilana. 'I'm sure we'll manage to cheer him up.'

'By the way, Mum,' said Aaron, 'I've got a favour to ask.' Aaron's big black eyes took on a well-rehearsed pleading look. 'Do you think Marcel could stay here while you're away?'

Marcel was Aaron's best friend and Sophie was very fond of him. He was seventeen, a year older than Aaron, and he fitted rather well into the family. A constant visitor, Marcel was Argentinian by birth and Sophie liked him because he was so charming and because he always tried to repay hospitality by washing the dishes. Sophie's children hated washing dishes. Although the children fought with each other, they never fought with Sophie and she suspected that the reason for this was that she never asked them to wash the dishes. Marcel was brought up differently. Marcel believed in housework. He was required to do almost all the housework in his home and this had become habitual. He found it almost impossible to stop his hands from picking up and tidying things. He looked at Sophie, almost with gratitude, when she asked him to do the washing-up. He could cook, too. Honey chicken was his specialty. He was ecstatic when she let him cook.

He spent a great deal of time at Sophie's house because his own family life had fallen apart. His parents had separated and he lived first with his mother, then with his father, then with his mother again.

'Please, Mum,' begged Aaron. 'He feels as if he can't bear to stay with either his mum or his dad at the moment.' Aaron and Marcel promised they would help Sophie by painting the walls, the ceiling and the cupboards of the newly renovated kitchen. Marcel would cook. Marcel would guarantee to do the housework while she was away. It seemed like a good bargain to Sophie. So she left them all there in the house; Jodie and Joseph and Marcel and her three children, Aaron, Paul and Ilana. It's a large house, tall and cool. Room enough for six people. And she left Jodie plenty of money to pay for food and petrol and entertainment. They all looked forward to enjoying a motherless adventure.

Sophie's father died eight days before she left for Nepal. The words look simple enough on the page but sometimes words are like granite.

When Michael left her, Sophie had not known how she was going to tell her parents. It was so embarrassing – to have failed again. She went over to Lindfield to visit them on her way to work. The car wasn't in the driveway. Perhaps her father had gone up the street to do some shopping. She let herself into the house. No one home. They must be playing bridge. She left a note for them on the bench in the kitchen.

Dear Mum and Dad,

I thought I'd better tell you that my relationship with Michael has ended. I thought I'd picked a good man this time but I was wrong.

Love

Sophie

When Sophie saw her parents the next weekend, her father looked at her with moist eyes and hugged her, but he said nothing. That was their way, never to mention anything upsetting.

Sophie had always thought her father walked through life with blinkers on, but perhaps she was wrong. Perhaps he saw everything quite clearly. Perhaps he just preferred to keep what he saw to himself. Sophie's father could see a sliver of blue in a sky full of rain. He never looked for people's faults; rather, he extracted and highlighted their virtues. Sophie did many things of which he disapproved, yet he never censured her.

The closest he ever came to criticizing her was when she was involved with an enormously aggressive and destructive man. He took her aside one day. 'Now, darling' he said, I wouldn't dream of making any comment about the way you live your life, but I just ask this of you. Don't let that man drive your car when the children are in it. Precious cargo, you know. We must look after them.'

He looked after everyone. He looked after his brother. He looked after his sister. He looked after his own mother until she died when he was sixty-five years old. He visited her one night during the week and took her out for a drive every Sunday afternoon. He looked after his children and then he looked after his grandchildren. He made each grandchild feel special and unique. He bought a house in Lindfield and built a swimming pool so that his children and grandchildren would enjoy visiting him. Every Saturday he would entertain six or eight grandchildren. The children would swim in the summer and be taken on outings during the winter. The parents would just drop the children there at ten o'clock on a Saturday morning and pick them up at five in the evening. After Sophie's divorce, her father picked up her children from school two afternoons a week and gave them afternoon tea and took them home, in order to make Sophie's teaching program more manageable. Sophie's mother, of course, played her part in all these activities but Sophie always had the feeling that her mother acquiesced in such happenings rather than initiating them.

He looked after Sophie. He bought all her children's clothes and shoes. He paid their kindergarten fees. He carpeted her house, replaced her washing machine, refrigerator, stove, clothes drier. He bought her new cars, on two different occasions, when he thought the one she owned needed replacement. He paid for her writing room to be constructed in the backyard. Michael designed and built it, but her father paid for the materials. When she went abroad for the first time, he gave her $1000 to spend. When she took her children overseas, four years later, he did the same thing. Once she lost her wallet. He insisted on knowing how much money she'd had in it and thrust $200 into her hand before she's had time to answer him. Every school holidays, he would slip a few hundred dollars into her bag. 'Just a little something to help you give the children a good time.' He was comfortably off, but he was not a wealthy man. His love and his generosity were boundless.

Sophie thought he would live forever.

Every morning, after Michael left, Sophie awoke with a sense of death. She was not afraid to die. Rather, she was aware of ageing, aware of the inevitability of death. The bed was empty and no man loved her and she was forty-five years old. When Michael was beside her, she lived with the sense that adventure lay ahead of her. When he went away he took the future with him. There was only blankness and emptiness and an awareness of decay that was intensified by the situation of her parents, over at Lindfield.

'She's getting worse every day,' Sophie's father said to her, on the phone. He was talking of her mother. 'Last night we were going out for dinner. We're waiting to be picked up. She's sitting there, in her fur coat, waiting. She'd even wrapped up a box of chocolates to take with us. Suddenly, up she gets and takes some chops out of the fridge and starts grilling them. What am I going to do?'

'Dad, you just have to be calm. She can't help it,' Sophie replied. 'You know what the doctor said. Her short-term memory's gone. She's going to get worse and worse. If you can't look after her, then we'll have to get some help for you.'

'No, no, darling. No, no. I can manage perfectly well.'

'Dad. You're eighty-two. No one expects you to look after her.'

'She can't cook any more. I mean, take today for instance. We're just having soup and hot bread rolls for lunch but she can't even manage that. She can't look after two things at the same time. What does she do? She burns the bread rolls to a cinder.'

'Dad, maybe you need someone to live in the house, someone to do the cooking and washing and that sort of thing.'

'No, no. I can't take those responsibilities away from her. She needs to believe that she can look after us. No, darling, I've decided that's the end of cooking. We're going to get our dinner every night from the gourmet takeaway and I'll help make breakfast and lunch.'

'Are you sure, Dad?'

'Yes, darling, I'm sure. The thing that's worrying me is this: what will I do when we can't go to the bridge club any more? I mean, everyone there is being so darned nice, but they're not going to put up with her forever. She can't remember the last move she's made. What'll happen to me then? I can't just stay here with her, day after day.'

'Can't you have friends over to play bridge?' Sophie suggested.

'That's no good any more. She gets anxious. She worries about having to make sandwiches.'

'Don't let her make them then,' said Sophie. 'Buy the sandwiches and cakes.'

'But she worries about when they're coming,' he complained. 'She asks me a hundred times a day. Is this the day that they're coming? What time are they coming? Should she make a cake? It's not worth the aggravation.'

'Why don't you take her out to the movies? You both like the movies.'

'She gets upset when she's away from the house. She opens and closes her handbag. She fiddles with her keys all the time. You can't enjoy yourself. You know she really wants to go home.'

Sophie would ring him or call in every day. Her brother and sister did the same. They invited their parents frequently to their houses for dinner. There was nothing they could do but wait for some indefinable, yet inevitable, catastrophe.

'No, Mummy darling,' he would say, with an edge of irritation in his voice, 'I've already told you we're not going to bridge today. Today is Tuesday. We don't go to bridge on Tuesdays. We go to bridge on Mondays and Wednesdays.'

How could he bear it? Sophie could not spend more than thirty minutes in her mother's company without feeling that she was going to scream. How could he listen to those same questions, over and over again?

'The thing that upsets me,' he said, with tears in is eyes, 'is that I lose my temper with her. And she does her best to be so nice to me. She warms my pyjamas every night on the electric blanket.'

Then it happened. A telephone call early in the morning. 'This darned silly thing's happened to me. Slipped in the shower. Stupid thing. Tiles must have been soapy. The doctor's just been. Two ribs broken. Could you send Mark over later to take Mummy up the street to get our dinner? I don't want to trouble anyone but we do need some more milk and a bit of fruit.'

Sophie took his car away. The doctor said he wouldn't be able to drive for five weeks and the only way of ensuring this was to remove the car. Mark used it and either he or Sophie called in every day to take them shopping or to drop them to bridge or to take them to the bank or just to make sure that they were alright.

Sophie looked at them with fear. What she had always regarded as indestructible was suddenly rendered vulnerable. She saw that they were going to die, that she was going to die, that the children were going to die. Death was everywhere. That's why, after six months of celibacy, she made herself find a new lover. She wanted to know that her body was still alive. The first time this man made love to her, she had an orgasm. He was rather pleased with himself. 'I don't want one orgasm,' she cried. 'One orgasm's no use to me. I need twenty.' She had so much death to counteract.

Sophie never gave her father back his car. He started to do strange things. He took her mother up to the hairdresser's on a Sunday morning and was amazed that the shop was closed. He went, by train, into the city on what he presumed to be the eve of the Day of Atonement only to find the gates of the Great Synagogue locked and barred. He went to the Lindfield travel agent and booked a world cruise on a Russian liner, on the assumption that he and his wife were perfectly capable of undertaking such a journey. He muddled days and dates. He gave Sophie a cheque dated years in advance. He would go to the bank at eight a.m. and, finding it closed, would complain to Sophie that there were more Sundays and public holidays than there used to be. He would take clothes to the dry-cleaners and forget to pick them up. He would lock himself out of the house. Always neat and meticulous he became disheveled and dirty. He did not shave or brush his hair. His tie was often stained with food.

Finally, he allowed them to get a nurse, on the understanding that it was Sophie's mother who needed constant attention.

They arranged for him to see a specialist, the same one who had assessed his wife's dramatic loss of memory. The doctor was infinitely kind. Sophie went into the surgery with him and her brother was there as well.

'Can you tell me what day it is today?' the doctor asked.

'Ah, well now, doctor, there you've got me. It might be Wednesday. Am I right? Is it Wednesday?' The doctor did not reply. Sophie's father must have known that he had made a mistake. She wanted to go to him and hug him and take him away and tell him that it didn't matter, it didn't matter one little bit what day it was.

'And the month?' the doctor probed. October. Late October. Surely he knew that. He'd celebrated his eighty-third birthday only a few weeks ago. Sophie conjured up all her love for him and all her energies and she tried to send him the word 'October'.

'April,' her father replied, 'the month is definitely April.'

'And who is the Prime Minister of Australia?' the doctor asked.

'That's easy,' he replied. 'It's Bob Hawke.'

'And what do you think of the state of affairs in Israel?'

'Difficult times. Very difficult times. Inflation is still so high.'

The questioning went on. When he answered correctly, Sophie wanted to applaud; when he displayed his absolute confusion, she plunged into despair. She felt that his very survival depended on giving correct answers. She wanted him to prove to the doctor and to her and to himself that there was nothing wrong with him at all.

The doctor decided that it would be good idea for him to go into hospital for ten days for rest and further testing. The tests showed deterioration of brain cells to be so extensive that the doctor was amazed that he had functioned so well for so long. In hospital he became so disoriented that they did not know whether he would be able to come back home. His hallucinations included imagining that the bed next to him was occupied by an Indian prince. However, he recovered his wits and came home. Twenty-four-hour nursing was necessary.

The worst thing was his tears.

'It's not fair,' he would weep. 'You work so darned hard all your life and just when you're ready to sit back and enjoy yourself, something like this happens.' He was talking of Sophie's mother, rather than of himself. What he meant was that his wife's mind had deteriorated so much that she couldn't go on a world cruise with him. He didn't accept his own decline. After all, he had kept a business going until he was eighty-one. He shared Sophie's view that he would live forever.

And then again, perhaps he did know that he was close to death. His speech became emotional and every word or sentiment brought tears to his eyes. He carried out sentimental acts. He took Ilana aside and, with tears flowing down her cheeks, he gave her $150 for her thirteenth birthday present, even though she had only recently turned twelve. Once she had told him she thought it unfair that Jewish boys received large gifts when they turned thirteen to mark their entry into manhood whereas girls who turned thirteen were not treated equally. He had promised that, when she turned thirteen, he would give her exactly the same present that he had given to each of her three big brothers.

'Spend the money, Ilana, just spend it on yourself. Don't save it,' he said as he pressed it into her hand. She could not kiss him. His tears disarmed her. She had to turn away.

He always advocated spending money rather than saving it. His wife and her sister had criticized him for that. They thought he gave too much away. They thought he should have put more money aside for his wife's future instead of squandering it on his children and grandchildren and, indeed, on perfect strangers if they he thought they needed his charity.

He called Aaron and Paul to him. He felt he might have favoured Mark because Mark was the oldest. He wanted to make sure that the other two boys did not feel neglected. He had two gold pens and he gave one to each of the boys, as a memento.

The best thing was that Sophie could hold his hand. So intense was his love for Sophie that she had never been comfortable about touching him. She would tolerate his hugs and kisses but she would have to move quickly away from his embrace, as if it were unseemly. Now the taboo no longer existed. She could hold his hand. His skin was silken to her touch and she could sit for hours with his hand softly in hers. Peace flowed between them.

Twenty-four-hour nursing was becoming too expensive. It could not be continued much longer. Sophie and her brother and sister had long discussions. What should they do? Should their parents go into a nursing home? Should their mother be moved? They were warned that, if their mother changed her environment, she would suffer a dramatic worsening of her condition. There were joys for them both at home; the garden, the swimming pool, the familiarity of possessions, the kindness of neighbours, the constant visits of children and grandchildren.

Sophie's father suffered a minor stroke and lost partial use of one leg and one hand. They knew he was dying but they did not know how long he would take to die. They found a wonderful girl, a nursing aide, who agreed to live in the house and look after their parents. She tended them day and night with great devotion.

'I wanted to live, to see how the children would grow up, to see what they would turn out to be,' he cried. 'It's not fair. There's something I have to tell you. I've lost my faith. After all these years of believing in God, suddenly it's all, all …'

'Oh, Dad, you've had a good life. You've been on trips overseas, you've had enough money to do as you please, you've succeeded in business, your children have all turned out alright and you've got eleven beautiful grandchildren. You've had a good life,' Sophie said to him.

They had a farewell dinner for Mark at the end of November, the day before he left for overseas. They had chicken schnitzel and potatoes, ice-cream and chocolate sauce – all things that Sophie's father loved. He had difficulty transferring the food from his plate to his mouth. Crumbs and drips constantly gathered on his chin. His face had to be wiped, as if he were a baby. Later, Sophie asked Mark whether he sensed that he would never see his grandpa again. 'No,' he replied, 'I thought he'd be completely better when I got back. There was something fresh and smooth about his face, he looked almost angelic.'

December began and Sophie became anxious about leaving for Nepal. She wanted her father to die before she left. They all wanted him to die. They could not bear to watch his disintegration. They wanted to remember the vigorous father, the active grandpa. They did not want to look at him like this.

On 14 December he had another stroke and he was put to bed. How well he timed it. He would not have wanted to spoil anyone's Christmas. He still knew everyone. He could still speak, at least enough to say their names. They all took turns to sit with him. He kept one hand permanently outstretched, as if he expected someone to hold it all the time. They obliged him.

The eighteenth was a Sunday. Aaron had to go to a friend's house to plan a holiday camping trip. Sophie dropped him there and came back home. She tried to get on with domestic tasks, changing beds, washing sheets, but she felt a mounting agitation. She rang Aaron and said, 'You'll have to finish your meeting. I have to go to Grandpa's. He's going to die. I'll pick you up in five minutes.' Ilana was afraid but Paul wanted to come with her. Sophie's father was humming in her head, buzzing in her head, whirling in her head and her need to be with him was a powerful call. She felt like a wild bird on the wing, her brain suffused with instinctual drive. Her agitation mounted; her heart pounded; she felt dizzy and light. They raced across to Lindfield, Sophie and her two precious boys.

'I just hope we can get there in time,' she cried and the boys were quiet but she could feel their hearts beating with hers.

She parked the car and flew into the house. Her aunt was there and her sister, her mother and the nurse. They were all drinking tea.

'There's no change,' said the nurse.

'I've just been in there and he's sleeping,' said Sophie's sister. 'Here, I'll pour you a cup of tea.'

She gave Sophie the tea and Sophie took one sip. Then she put it down. 'I'll just go in and take a look at him,' she said. She walked down the hall and into her parents' bedroom. He was lying on his side, curled up like a baby. She could hear his laboured breathing as she walked into the room. The air smelled of urine. She went round to the side of the bed. His hand was black. She sat down on the bed and she held his hand. She watched his breath. It was tortuous and hard – in, out, in, out. Twice only. And then it stopped. Just like that. She turned around and saw that Aaron had followed her into the room. He knew, as surely as she did, that he had to be there. An instant later, Paul came in.

'He's dead, Paul,' she said. Paul turned sharply away and put his hand over his face. 'No,' she said, 'don't be afraid. Come and see. He looks so peaceful.' Sophie let go her father's hand and she brushed her lips to his forehead. His eyes were closed and his skin felt cool. She had never met death before. It was nothing to fear.

They went out of the room, Sophie and her sons. The others were all chatting, drinking tea. The phone rang and Sophie's sister answered it. It was their brother.

'I think he's dead,' said Sophie and they all stopped talking. Sophie's mother did not fully understand but the others all agreed that it was right that Sophie had been with him at the moment of his death. They did not feel sadness. What they felt was relief. There were no tears. Sophie found two twenty-cent coins beside her father's bed. He had left them there to be placed over his eyes. He had lost his faith but not his sense of tradition.

Sophie felt euphoric. She felt a sense of rightness because she had been the one to be with her father when he died. A fitting ending to their relationship.

Sophie and the children decided that Grandpa would not have wanted them to be unhappy and they set off that evening to celebrate his passing in a manner that he would have regarded as entirely suitable. They picked up Jodie so that she could accompany them to their wake at the Gelato Bar at Bondi.

There was Aaron and Marcel, Paul and Ilana, Jodie and Sophie. They ate chocolate torte and hazelnut torte and cheese-cake and various flavours of gelato. They were all quite high. After they'd finished stuffing themselves with cakes, they didn't want to go home. They had too much energy, so they decided to go for a walk along the beach. They took off their shoes and they pranced and danced and jumped their way along the sand until they came to the northern end of the beach. They waded through the children's swimming pool and climbed up onto the rocks. They settled themselves down and looked out to sea.

'I haven't cried yet, you know,' said Ilana. 'I'm not really sad. After all, I was expecting it.'

'Probably some day, in about twenty years' time, you'll find yourself sitting somewhere and you'll cry for your Grandpa,' said Jodie.

Ilana slid a confiding glance in Sophie's direction, the kind of look that said, 'What on earth is she on about?' Sophie sent a reassuring look back to Ilana.

'There's no reason in the world why you should cry,' Sophie said. 'He had a happy life. He was never sick until the last few months and he died with the people he loved all around him.'

Jodie sat in front of Sophie. She had her legs bent and her arms around her knees. Marcel and Paul sat close to her, one on each side. Aaron and Ilana and Sophie were behind them. Suddenly Jodie stood up and spread out her arms and reached up towards the sky.

'Look out there, children, way out there, as far as you can into the sky. Can you feel it? Grandpa's soul is here and it's longing to fly away, away into eternity. Stand up now and let yourselves feel his soul flying away. Say goodbye to him as he goes. We are all one. We are all part of the cosmos. We have different bodies but our souls at death become part of the universe, part of the essence of all things.'

Aaron rolled his eyes at Sophie as if to say, 'Listen to her! She must be mad.'

'I haven't got a soul,' Sophie declared firmly. 'I've just got a body and when I die, that'll be the end of me. I'm sure of that.'

'Me too,' chirped Ilana, like her mother, a total pragmatist.

How can you be so sure?' said Paul. 'You've no right to say that to us.' Sophie could see that he was getting upset. 'I think there's something. I don't know what it is. There might be a God. You know I have dreams that turn out to be true. You know I have strange, unexplained experiences, so why do you think you're so right?'

'Jodie's right,' said Marcel. 'There is a soul. There is a spirit. There is a God. What does life mean if you can't feel yourself to be part of the spiritual essence of all things?'

They were forming themselves into battle lines. Sophie could see that the situation could become unpleasant and she didn't want that to happen.

'I'm sick of all this crap,' said Aaron. 'I want to go home.' So, disgruntled and irritable, they got up and started to walk back towards the car.

As they walked back along the beach, Sophie felt disappointed that the sense of harmony and well-being had been disrupted. She was irritated with Jodie for attempting to add a spiritual dimension to her father's death and even more irritated with herself for being childish enough to take up the argument. A few moments later Sophie saw Jodie put her arm around Marcel's shoulders. Marcel looked at her and smiled and responded by putting his arm around her waist. Perhaps Jodie felt that Marcel was upset and needed mothering or perhaps they were holding onto each other because, at this particular moment, neither of them felt as if they were real members of Sophie's family.

The funeral was held two days later. Over two hundred people crowded the Chevra Kadisha at Woollahra, the measure of Sophie's father's capacity to evoke respect and love. Sophie and the children wore their brightest clothes. People came up to her with long faces and serious eyes and she found it difficult to suppress laughter in the face of conventional portrayals of sadness.

'Don't they understand?' Aaron said to Sophie, his irrepressible black eyes shining with joy. 'Grandpa was about life and joy and being happy. He wouldn't want us to cry. He'd be telling me to make the most of my life, to get out there and have a good time.'

Women have no role to play at Jewish funerals, but all the women and girls in the family turned up at the cemetery. Except for Sohpie's mother. They thought it better for her to stay at home with her sister. After the ceremony at the graveside, the men lined up to tip the ritual three shovels of dirt onto the coffin. Sophie's brother went first; then her oldest cousin. As she stood there, her heart began to pound and she was compelled to break into the line of men and grab the shovel and shaking, shaking from head to toe, she shovelled dirt into her father's grave. She expected the rabbi, or even God himself, to intervene at this appalling breaking of tradition, but nothing happened. She knew the children would be proud of her.

Afterwards they went back to Sophie's mother at the house at Lindfield. All her children and all her grandchildren, except for Mark, away in England. They bought barbecued chickens and salads from Goldy's Gourmet food shop. They sat around the swimming pool. They ate and drank and laughed and then they swam in relay races.

Late in the afternoon, they went home. All the euphoria of the last few days fell away and a sadness suffused the house. A pervading melancholy seized hold of Sophie and continued throughout the week until her departure for Nepal.

Traditionally, Christmas day had always been spent at Lindfield, but the thought of doing that was now distasteful so everyone came to Sophie's house instead. They did their best but nothing was the same. They were all aware of the absence of Sophie's benign and beautiful father. It was the end of an era.

The next day Sophie left for Nepal. As soon as she stepped onto the plane she was able to shut the children away and, with excitement and enthusiasm, she thrust herself into adventure.

One night in Bangkok, one night in Katmandu and then off on a twenty-one day trek.

Sophie, of course, survived this arduous undertaking but she did not learn anything about spiritual fulfilment. In fact, the journey was entirely a physical one and lacked any mystical dimension. The majestic Himalayas failed to raise anything more in Sophie than a sense of awe and wonder.

She damaged her leg on the second day of the trek and had to drag on, very painfully, for another two days until they reached the little mountain village of Simagon where she was left with a Nepalese family for a week while the other members of her trekking party went on and upwards to greater heights.

She was very lucky to have been left behind because she had the opportunity of getting to know some real Nepalese people and she had time to think. One day, while sitting at the top of the mountain in the sun, gazing at the magnificent Himalayas, she came quite close to what others might regard as a moment of spiritual insight. She suddenly began to weep; for her father, for Michael, for all the losses over all the years. This, together with the simplicity of the way of life around her, somehow cleansed and purified her. She felt vigorous and strong and free. She felt she could face whatever life might have in store for her.

She walked and exercised and massaged her injured leg so that, by the time the other participants of the trekking party had returned, she felt fit enough to continue. With the help of a cane staff and a friendly Sherpa, she was able to walk five or six hours a day, up and down 600 metre mountains and over snow-driven 4000 metre passes. She felt an enormous sense of achievement at having faced and overcome such a difficult physical challenge.

By the time she got back to Katmandu, Sophie had begun to miss the children and this feeling rapidly grew into an impatient longing to see their faces again. The flight home seemed interminable; the delay through Customs unwarranted; and it was with a great sense of relief that she emerged through the doors to the familiar cries of, 'Mummy! Here we are! Over here!' She hugged the children and she hugged Jodie and they all hopped into the car. On the way home, Sophie told them all about her adventures in Nepal.

As soon as they got inside the house, Sophie undid her pack and distributed the presents she had bought for them all. While they were busily engaged in unwrapping and examining their new possessions, Sophie asked 'Well, how did you all get on while I was away?'

'We'll talk about that another time, Sophie,' Jodie replied. Sophie imagined that a few minor problems had arisen and that Jodie, very kindly, was allowing her to enjoy her homecoming before telling her about them.

'Did you have enough money? Do I owe you anything, Jodie? Here, let me give you an extra fifty dollars.'

'No, Mum,' said Ilana, trying on a new Nepalese bracelet. 'Give her an extra hundred because she looked after us so well.'

Jodie took the money, collected her things and went off home to her flat in Manly. She did not say goodbye to the children. The children all seemed a bit subdued and pretended to be totally absorbed in their presents. Joseph emerged briefly from his room to welcome Sophie and to tell her that he knew Mark would be back shortly and that he had arranged to leave the house in a few days' time. He would stay with friends until he could arrange something more permanent for himself. She was relieved that Joseph did not seem to be any worse than he was when she went away. She looked again at the children. Something was wrong but Sophie did not want to pursue the matter. She felt jet-lagged and ill. She'd had an irritating cough for the last week and every time she breathed it felt as if the air seared the entire inside surface of her lungs.

It wasn't until three days later, when she was having dinner with the children in a little Malaysian restaurant at Crows Nest, that they gave her the first inkling of what had happened while she was away. Sophie did not want to listen to what they were saying because listening would mean the acceptance of responsibility, listening would mean the burden of guilt. So Sophie sat patiently and allowed the children to speak and, although she heard what they were saying, she could not permit herself to acknowledge all the implications behind the words. She absorbed enough to realize that Jodie could no longer play any part in their lives.

Sophie was not ready to face the entire truth because the school year was beginning and she needed all her energies to get through first term. There were new classes to meet and new texts to prepare. When Mark started university, he didn't like it at all. Sophie had told him how exciting it would be to do an Arts degree at Sydney University, but Mark found the whole thing very boring. Sophie had to spend a great deal of time talking to him, helping him, encouraging him to keep attending. There was the endless domestic routine of shopping, cooking, washing, ironing, driving the children here and there. In addition there was the escalating worry of what to do about Sophie's mother who was deteriorating rapidly but still living at Lindfield with a nurse.

By the May holidays, however, things had settled down. Mark had made friends and now found university bearable because he enjoyed the social life and Sophie's mother had been moved to a nursing home. Sophie now felt ready to learn all the details of what had happened to the children while she was away in Nepal. Not a word had been heard from Jodie. She had not, at any time, attempted to contact Sophie in order to give her own account of the events. So she told the children that she wanted each of them to tell her, one by one, exactly what had happened.

Aaron wanted to be first so he and Sophie went down to the writing room in the backyard.

'I sort of know what happened, Aaron,' said Sophie, 'but I want to understand it properly. I'm not going to ask you any questions. You just tell me about it in your own way.'

'Look,' said Aaron,' the first thing you ought to know is that I didn't feel bad about your going away. I realised you needed to go away. The only loss I felt was that Grandpa had died and the whole of my life had changed. Something that had always been there wasn't there any longer.

'That's why I was pretty upset that night at Bondi Beach. There we were, down at the beach, each of us trying to handle how we felt and Jodie started talking all this crap about the stars and eternity. She was trying to get everyone to see Grandpa's death in terms of some deep, universal, spiritual significance. And that gave me the shits. It had nothing to do with her. He was my Grandpa and I'd known him for so long, for all of my life. Grandpa had died that very day and I'd been there with you. I'd watched him die. I felt the loss. So what right did she have to tell me how I should feel? Her spiritual views had nothing to do with me. She was trying to put his death into terms that weren't relevant to me. So I got the shits and I said to you, remember I said, "Let's go," because I didn't like what she was saying. That's why I wanted to leave.

'And then we started walking back along the beach and Marcel and Jodie put their arms around each other and I thought, Well this is funny. Fancy Marcel flirting with Jodie. I wasn't really surprised because Marcel flirts with just about everyone. You know what he's like. He even flirts with people's mothers. And I thought, Oh, yes, here we go again. At the time, that night on the beach, it didn't register with me that they were really interested in each other. I thought it was a joke. The main thing on my mind was that my Grandpa had just died.

'They always flirted, especially when we went out. They'd put their arms around each other. Only it seemed to me that Marcel had become a bit more captivated than he wanted to be. Usually, when Marcel flirts with people, he's on top, he dominates. It was different this time. I could see it was getting serious.

'The main problem was the reaction it evoked in Ilana. Every time they flirted, Ilana would scream, "Stop it! You look disgusting," but they took no notice of her. They went on doing whatever it was they were doing. Ilana would storm out of the room, or shout, or scream, or throw something, or do something bitchy. At first I didn't really understand why Ilana was reacting so violently. I just knew, instinctively, that I had to become her ally. I had to help her because Jodie wasn't doing her job. Jodie had been like a sister to Ilana; Jodie was supposed to be taking your place as Ilana's mother and here she was, creating terrible problems for the person she was meant to look after. I knew that, whatever happened, I had to look after Ilana and take her side.

'It was alright when Joseph was there. Of course Joseph spent most of his time down in his room, but whenever he emerged, he was very nice to Ilana. But whenever anyone else was around it was terrible. There was a lot of conflict between Ilana and Marcel, and Jodie always took Marcel's side. The conflict mostly arose over keeping the house tidy. When you left, Jodie and Marcel decided to impose an order onto the house that was quite alien to us. Marcel especially. I suppose he couldn't help it. His father's a cleaner; it's in-built into his nature. Nevertheless, he used his favour in Jodie's eyes to become very bossy. He would expect us to be grateful to him but we would just say, "Where the fuck did you put this? Where the fuck did you put that?" I thought Marcel was taking on too big a role in our house over this matter of tidiness. He was staying there as a favour and he'd gone too far. The more he ran around cleaning up, the more Ilana and Paul and I would try to mess it up again. We were trying to keep the house the way we like it, you know, homely and lived-in. He was really hurt when Ilana wouldn't thank him for his efforts. Instead she'd say, "Fuck off, you bastard."

'Once he took me aside and said, "Look, if she's going to behave like a little kid, then I'm going to treat her like one." And I said, "But she is a little kid, she's only twelve years old!" and he said, "Well I don't care." The trouble is that Ilana is so mature in some ways that people expect too much of her. Marcel couldn't see that his enchantment with Jodie was hurting Ilana. He always used to flirt with Ilana. He meant it as a joke but I think she took him seriously. I'm sure she felt attracted to Marcel and she must have felt he betrayed her by flirting with Jodie. So Ilana just reacted blindly, to express her outrage.

'I don't understand it, you know. Jodie lived so peacefully in our house for so long. Her role in our family was to defuse explosive situations and yet, here she was, creating chaos. I mean, for nine years we'd known her. For all that time we'd seen her as a peace-maker. And yet the minute she was in a position of authority, she changed.

'She betrayed your trust in so many ways. She drove the car stoned; she smoked dope in the house. She even made Ilana watch television in your bedroom while she and her friends smoked in the lounge-room. Ilana would say things to Jodie like, "Oh, don't do that. Mum wouldn't like it," and Jodie would say, "Well, your mother's not here now," and Ilana would say, "I think you should follow the rules that Mum makes for this house," and Jodie would reply, "Well, I'm in charge now, Ilana, and I'll make the rules." It was horrible. You know how Ilana can't stand the smell of marijuana. Jodie knew that too but she didn't care. That infuriated me but what could I say? People came into the house and smoked and I just had to watch. Marcel smoked with them as well and he knew how I felt. He knew the rules. No smoking in the house. I was furious but I felt helpless. I think it was really slack of Jodie to do things like that behind your back. To my mind Jodie really betrayed all the trust you put in her when you said, "Can you look after the kids for me?"

'Of course, I should have known. I knew there was that other side of her, the part of her that was involved with drugs. I knew her better than you did. I mean, when she lived with us we kept her sane and calm. That whole time she lived with us she was celibate and she never used any drugs, but from the moment she moved into her flat at Manly, she got involved with those people again. She used to talk to me about her problems on the way to our tai chi lessons. She kept telling me how sick she was. I'd say, "Look, don't complain to me about it. You know as well as I do that if you're going to do tai chi properly you've got to stop taking drugs. Smoking dope just buggers up your immune system. That's why you're sick."

'She couldn't take it when I gave her advice. She'd say things to me like, "Look, talk to me in fifteen years' time." That really used to give me the shits because I was sixteen and she was thirty-two and I knew myself a hell of a lot better than she knew herself. She thought I was young and immature but I tell you what, considering her age and stage of life, I was a lot more mature than she was. She knew that and she resented it. I always thought it was very symbolic, very true somehow, that she chose to wear rose-tinted glasses.

'She'd only been in that flat in Manly for four weeks before you went away to Nepal. Four weeks. That's all it took for her to lose all that she'd gained by staying with us. You see, you keep this place under control and when you're here she can be part of that order, but when you went away she couldn't be you. She had to try to impose her own kind of order and she had no sort of control over her own life. So if she had no control over herself, how was she going to exercise control over anyone else? I could see all this and I was the oldest member of the family here and I knew I had to keep things together.

'I had to organise a lot of things. Going out with Dad, for instance. When we were all supposed to go out with Dad, I'd somehow manage to get everyone in the right place at the right time. And she'd say, "Wow, Aaron, you did that really well," and I'd say, "Well, what did you expect?" I was pissed off that she was surprised at the way I managed to keep things together. And the shopping. She was hopeless at that. And she couldn't cook. Marcel did all the cooking. We had so much fucking honey chicken. I was always buying chickens and Marcel was always cooking them. Jodie didn't do much more than dole out the money and she didn't do that particularly well. I could have coped much better than she did. It's just that you needed to be able to drive. If only I'd been seventeen. If only I'd had a licence. None of this would have happened.

'I didn't just feel she betrayed you. I felt she betrayed me. I felt I'd become her real friend over the time I'd been doing tai chi with her and she seemed to sweep my friendship aside. It was all because of Marcel. She put her feelings for him before everything else, before family commitment and that was wrong and that's why I can never forgive her.

'You know, Jodie didn't just flirt with Marcel. She flirted with all of us. One day we were all in your bedroom and she said, "Give me a massage." She lay down naked on your bed and we all had to massage her. If that's not flirting with all of us, what is? I mean, she's lying there naked and here's all these little boys rubbing her. I think that's pretty weird. She wouldn't have done that if you'd been home, now would she? Of course she'd give all of us massages too but then that's her occupation. At first Paul and I were massaging her and Ilana too. She didn't want Marcel to come in. Maybe she thought he'd get too excited but we made him massage her as well.

'Whenever she massaged me, she'd say things like, "Does that make it hard?" and that would make me feel sick. I paid her back in the end. Just before you came back from Nepal. By that time she was really very confused and depressed. She was lying down on your bed one day, pretending to be asleep and I decided to flirt with her. I stroked her head and then I got up and walked away and she said, "Aaron, I can't, you're my brother," and I said, "Oh, I don't think that matters as long as it feels good." I went out of the room and I felt pleased with myself because I knew I'd created an enormous conflict for her. She couldn't handle it. I didn't want to sleep with her. She revolted me.

'She never slept with Marcel but she did want to. She said that he was a flirt and that, by flirting with him, she was teaching him a lesson but I knew what it was all about. She really wanted Marcel and, after a while, I found it did reach the stage where I was sickened. It seemed to me to be unnatural and revolting. I started to see her as a slut. Probably she was genuinely attracted to young boys. She desired us and felt it was wrong to act out that desire so she played with it and she played with us and, in the process, she became disturbed and confused.

'Paul felt it too. He had this wonderfully graphic dream about us all having to fuck Jodie and we opened her legs and there was all this steam and maggots and this stuff pouring out of her cunt and he woke up in horror.

'The flirtation between Jodie and Marcel created conflicts between me and Marcel. We started fighting about all sorts of things, especially about how the kitchen should be painted. I knew a lot more about painting than he did but he would always stir me and the tension built up and up. Finally we had a big fight about how to paint the ceiling and I told him to leave. I told him to fuck off. So he packed up all his things and he started to leave and I said to him, "Well, you can't leave because you've got nowhere to go. But when we're painting, you've got to do what I say. I'm not going to take any of your shit." So we finished the painting but you know how annoyed you can get when a friend is around for too long.

'I was worried about going away camping and leaving Ilana undefended but she solved the problem by going to stay with her friend, Christine. The camping was great and Paul and

Marcel stayed at Manly with Jodie while I was away. Then we went off to Terrigal for a week with Dad. Paul and his friend and Marcel and me. It was a good week and I was friendly with Marcel again because we were far away from the conflict at home. Ilana was still staying at Christine's so I didn't feel too worried about her. I could really just relax and enjoy myself.

'But when we got back from Terrigal, I found that Ilana had been chucked out of Christine's house. I guess she'd outgrown her welcome. After all, she'd been staying with them for two weeks. She's had to go and stay with Jodie at Manly and Jodie had given her an awful time. Jodie complained to me. She told me Ilana had been behaving like an absolute bitch but I just said, "Well, Jodie, you must have done something to hurt her. Ilana's not just going to attack you for nothing."

'Those last few days at home, just before you came back, were terrible. Jodie and Ilana weren't talking to each other. Jodie decided that the house had to be tidied up. It was a last, desperate effort on her part to impose some kind of order. Marcel helped her but I wouldn't have anything to do with it. I couldn't see that you would mind if the house was as untidy when you got back as it had been when you went away. I thought you would really expect to find it much as you had left it. Besides, she was only putting things into surface order; underneath, everything had fallen apart.

'She alienated herself from Joseph, too, in the end. I remember that last morning, when we were getting ready to pick you up from the airport. Jodie was trying to ring up to find out if the plane was on time. Joseph was on the downstairs phone. Jodie ordered him to get off the phone, that she was trying to ring the airport. He stormed up the stairs and exploded, "What do you think you're doing?" he shouted. "Don't do it again!

Don't do it again!" This really quiet, withdrawn guy, you know, shouting and shouting at her. We all laughed and she started crying. She drove to the airport like a madwoman. We couldn't look at each other. We knew that if we looked at each other we might start laughing and if we laughed Jodie might have an accident. Not a word spoken all the way to the airport. Quiet hysteria, that's what I'd call it.

'It's been a time of total change, really, and that change began with Grandpa's death. A stage in our lives had come to an end. You know, Mum, if I think about it, those four weeks you were away in Nepal seem like the longest four weeks I've ever known.'

When Aaron finished talking, Sophie smiled at him. 'Well, Aaron, you'll be seventeen next week. You'll have your driving licence soon.'

'It's a bit late, though, isn't it? That's what I kept thinking all the time you were away. If only I'd had my licence none of this would ever have happened. I could have looked after everyone.'

The next day Marcel came over to the house to watch videos with Aaron, and Sophie asked him if he'd mind talking to her for a while.

'No, I don't mind at all,' said Marcel. 'Aaron told me you wanted me to tell you my views on what happened while you were away. I've been thinking and thinking about it, these last three or four months, sorting it all out in my own mind. I'd really like to tell someone about it.'

On the way down to the writing room Sophie said, 'I thought you might be embarrassed to talk to me about it.'

'No, no,' Marcel insisted. 'You know I've always been able to talk to you. I really do want to tell you all about it. Sophie, you can't imagine how much I looked forward to staying in

67

your house. I wanted to belong there. I felt I wasn't wanted by my mother or my father and I felt a great need to be part of a family. Your house, you know, is so open and friendly. I thought I'd have no difficulty in finding my place there. And I've always seen your house as a great challenge. I thought how good it would be to take over all the cleaning chores and bring it all into order. I thought I could do it, all by myself.

'I didn't expect any opposition. I thought the others would be pleased but they resented everything I tried to do. It was pretty hard to take because I thought I was doing the right thing. You see, I was staying in your house and your money was feeding me and supporting me and I felt I had to repay you for that. Cooking wasn't enough. I'd promised you I'd clean the house and they wouldn't let me do that. I thought that, no matter what I said when you got back, you'd blame me if the house wasn't clean and tidy. I didn't want you to think badly of me.

'I couldn't understand why Ilana kept screaming at me. She was very angry, very irrational. She was so bitchy and that really hurt me because I cared as much about her as I did about everyone else in the house. I didn't realize that Ilana took my flirting seriously. You know what I'm like. I joke around. That's all my flirting was with Ilana – just playing around. I think she knows that now.

'I want to tell you about Jodie. You know, when I was first introduced to Jodie, I thought she was a really laid-back person. She seemed to be so much with the times. I looked up to her because she kept coming out with deep, philosophical thoughts that my mind had never thought of. I was terribly impressed. And spiritual ideas, too. I remember that night we went to Bondi Beach and she told us to relax and stare into the horizon, to project ourselves as far away as we could, out into the darkness, just to let ourselves go. It was like escaping. And I needed to escape. I'd just been involved in my first homosexual experience. I'd had to leave home. I was confused and I didn't know what was going to happen to me. She was showing me how to go away from my problems and I was grateful.

'I was rather surprised, at first, when she started flirting with me. I didn't know how to take it. I had to take it as a joke because, if I'd taken it seriously, I wouldn't have known what to do. But I liked it, too. It was flattering. It was good for my ego. Here I was, being chased by an older woman.

'She didn't flirt just with me. After you left, she started flirting with Aaron and Paul. It was her chance to really go for it. Here she was with a house full of boys. And then, you see, Ilana became a threat. Ilana was female and she was young. She was somehow innocent, non-sexual. She was the opposite of Jodie. That's what it was all about. Jodie's attraction to young boys was an attempt to be youthful. That's why she was so horrible to Ilana. Ilana was what Jodie wanted to be and Ilana was judging Jodie very severely.

'The thing that stands out most in my mind was the day of the big massage at Jodie's place, at Manly, when just Paul and I were staying there. She'd been teaching us all how to massage and she'd been telling Paul and me how important it was to practise massage if we wanted to be any good at it. She said she'd ask her flatmate, Rani, if we boys could practise on her. Then Jodie came out of the room and said, "She'll be ready in a minute." Paul and I walked in and she was naked on the massage table. You know, usually you have underwear on or a towel or something but no, there she was, just lying there naked, her arms and legs spread apart and her body sort of asking us to give her a massage. Paul and I tried to ignore everything and practise our massage but somehow we got onto the subject of sex and Paul and I started talking about the frigid test.

"What's that?" she asked.

"Well," we explained, "a man runs his finger down your body from your forehead and you have to tell him when to stop."

"Try it on me," Rani said, "and let's see if it works." So Paul and I were running our fingers from her forehead down as far as … we thought she was going to freak out when we got to her belly button or something … but no, we found ourselves going down further and further and Paul and I were looking at each other with looks that were saying, "Let's stop!" and we had to stop. But she didn't stop us. She wanted us to go on but we couldn't. She was enjoying herself. And that night Paul and I … we couldn't stop talking about it … all night, you know. We stayed as close as possible to each other.

'I thought that Jodie would sleep with me. I thought about it lots of times but whenever I thought about it I would remind myself that my mother was about the same age as Jodie and I would say to myself, "No, no!" Anyway, Jodie wasn't the best looking person in the world.

'And then, of course, she brought her boyfriend to the flat. I didn't know she had a boyfriend. He had one front tooth missing and I wondered how she could go out with someone who looked like that. If she was attracted to people like me and Paul, then how could she be attracted to a man with one front tooth missing? I decided she must be joking, joking with all of us. I felt better thinking that. If she wasn't serious, then I didn't have to get involved and I didn't have to feel frightened. Her boyfriend only came to the flat once while we were staying there. They left Paul and me alone while they went into the kitchen to talk and then they went into the bedroom for a long time. Paul and I sat in the lounge-room and felt as if we were in a house where we didn't belong.

'During the week that we stayed at Manly, we used to get up early in the morning, the three of us, and go to the beach and have a swim. Sometimes I didn't go. You know what I'm like. I think I look too fat in my swimming costume so sometimes I didn't go with them. Then I'd stay home and I'd imagine Jodie and Paul swimming naked under the water. When they came back from the beach I knew that nothing like that had really happened but I wished, at those times, that I could have been a grain of sand on the beach, just watching them.

'Late at night we used to go back out on to the beach. We would run the entire length of the beach and write words to do with love in big letters on the sand and we would draw gigantic butterflies and sit down and watch the water wash them away. We'd all think how sad that was and how terrible, you know, that the world we'd made would be washed away.

'Rani didn't come out with us but she was often in the flat and when she was there we'd have cups of coffee and talk. I got on well with Rani. Sometimes I'd be sitting in the lounge-room with Paul and the doorbell would ring. Rani would answer it and she would take a man into her bedroom and then, about an hour later, escort him out. Then the doorbell would ring again and another man would come and she'd take him into her bedroom. They were all Orange people and apparently they're allowed to sleep with anyone in their group. That's what being an Orange person is all about. Paul and I would sit there thinking, this is pretty good. No guilt. Here one day, gone the next. Plenty of sex. We thought it would be fun to be an Orange person.

'And then we went on that holiday to Terrigal. Aaron and I were good friends again and we had heaps of fun. Down at the beach there were a lot of rocks. There was a sort of rock platform reaching out to the sea and, at the end of it, there were broken rocks, some of them very large. Big waves would crash against these rocks and, every morning, Aaron and I used to sit on the rock furthest from the land. We'd somehow get out there and hold on as tight as we could and let the biggest waves hit us. Our legs would be bruised and sometimes bleeding from where they scratched against the rocks. It was terrifying. That was the good thing about it. It was a challenge – not to be taken away by the waves. The last time we went there a gigantic wave broke right over our heads. We couldn't breathe. We lost our grip. Somehow we managed to get out of the water. We never went back.

'It was a great relief being up there at Terrigal. We were boys again, playing, fighting, meeting challenges. Then we had to go back home. Aaron and I started fighting again, and I felt I had to leave the house before you got back. I could see I was getting in the way. I couldn't help cleaning; Ilana kept scream-ing at me; Jodie was giving me the shits and Aaron was bitter. So I left. Aaron rang me at Mum's place to tell me you were coming back but he said there was no room for me in the car. That's why I didn't go out to the airport to meet you. I was sure that you would blame me for everything that had gone wrong.

'Joseph was important. Not to the others, perhaps, but he was to me. This disturbed homosexual, spending all day in a dark, silent room. That was the point, you see, because I was confused about my sexuality. I'd had this homosexual flirtation and I didn't know where such a thing might lead me. Did homosexuality lead to madness, I wondered? And I felt I was going mad, I really did. I needed that relationship with Jodie; I needed to hold onto it because I felt so alone. You understand that, don't you? I know I caused a lot of the bad feeling that went on in the house while you were away but I couldn't help what I was doing. I had such a great and terrible need to belong somewhere. Sophie, I have to know, do you blame me for what happened?'

'No, Marcel, I don't think it was your fault.' Sophie thought that if she blamed anyone it would have to be herself. After hearing what Aaron and Marcel had to say, she accepted the fact that there was a side to Jodie that Sophie had never seen, but why had she never seen it? Sophie came to the conclusion that she had constructed her own image of Jodie over the years and even if she had observed behaviour that did not coincide with this image, she would certainly have chosen to ignore it.

Ilana had already indicated that she wanted to be the last to tell her story because, she insisted, hers would be the best and it is always wise to save the best for last. So Sophie spoke to Paul next. Because of Paul's vagueness, his absent-mindedness and his capacity to switch off in an instant, other members of the family sometimes thought he didn't notice things but Sophie knew that he would have watched and observed everything that was going on and she was eager to hear what he had to say.

'I've been thinking about what happened,' said Paul, 'and the strange thing is that I was outside of it all. I was watching but I wasn't really involved.

'I trusted Jodie absolutely. I believed everything she said to me and I probably still would. I believed all that she told me about spiritual matters and I trusted her advice in everyday matters as well. If there was something wrong with me, she'd say, "Do this," and I'd know that whatever she told me to do would be right. That time I hurt my finger playing judo, she told me how to make it feel better. It was simple, just to put my hand in hot water and then in freezing water, but it worked. You wouldn't have told me to do that. You'd have told me to take an aspirin. I trusted what she had to say as an adult because she'd been around me since I was a little boy. I hope that she'll come back to our family and, if she does, I'll trust her again.

'Everyone else feels bitter towards her but I don't. I thought Aaron and Ilana were wrong in turning against her but I can see that they had their own individual reasons for feeling that she betrayed them. I just never shared those feelings.

'I don't think she intended any harm. She was lonely and depressed and I think her flirtation with Marcel was just an attempt to make herself feel happier. I couldn't feel bitter towards her because I felt sorry for her.

'She was certainly serious about Marcel. That week, when we were staying with her at Manly, Marcel and I slept on the water bed. In the morning, she'd come in and lie next to him and put her arm around him and touch him and it was obvious that she felt something for him.

'That first morning, I wasn't sure whether I should stay in the room or leave. Marcel motioned to me to stay but I misinterpreted his gesture. I thought he was saying, "Go away," so I went out of the room. When I came back I could tell that nothing had happened but Marcel was petrified. He was lying there like a frightened duck. He said, "Don't go, don't go." Until that time I thought he was interested in Jodie, but after that I realized he was scared. He wanted me to protect him.

'So much happened during the week at Manly. It seemed much longer than a week. I was writing a lot of poetry myself so it was a good time for me in that way. Marcel and I spent a lot of time together, just the two of us, talking, going to the beach. You know, I'd always thought of Marcel as a real Casanova but I found out that he was totally different from my view of him. I thought he was a very mature person who wouldn't be affected by the sort of situation he found himself in with Jodie. I thought he was more god-like than he is. I'd seen him perform on stage with such assurance and certainty. I really looked up to him. I don't mean that I lost respect for him during the week at Manly, but I found out that he was not much different from myself. He was discovering his sexuality just as I was discovering mine and, although he's three years older than me, he was just as scared as I was.'

'Of course, he's different from me because he's confused about his sexual direction. That's probably why he was so frightened by the advances Jodie made. He would make homosexual gestures towards me but I could not tell to what extent he was serious so I thought it wiser to treat such things as a joke. I didn't really know what was happening to him but I could certainly tell that he was confused.

'There was so much sexuality over there at Manly. Those Orange people! It didn't shock me because I was used to seeing naked people. I sort of laughed. I mean, Marcel and I might be sitting there on the couch and Rani would walk in naked. One time, I was sitting in a chair in Jodie's room facing the bathroom. Rani went in there and had a shower with the door open. I think she was showing off a bit. One day Marcel and I gave Rani a massage. "Do whatever you want. I don't mind." That's what she said. Marcel was a bit taken aback. We kept looking at each other and laughing and trying to hide our erections under our towels. It seems funny when you think of boys, teenage boys, wanting to do sexual things and you think of the girl being the one to say no. Here everything was reversed. The girl was willing. She was encouraging us to go on but we weren't taking the opportunity she offered us. It was strange because, when we were alone, we'd talk about sex and how great it would be to have sex with Rani but when it came to it we were scared and we didn't do anything much at all. I wanted to and he wanted to but we sort of couldn't. So we just massaged her breasts and that was great but we couldn't go any further.

'It was good that week at Manly. We got away from home and away from the problems that had existed there between Jodie and Ilana. I thought both Jodie and Ilana were being pretty childish but I wasn't going to take sides. I didn't think I should because I didn't know who was right and who was wrong.

'I know the others think she spent too much of your money and that she didn't manage things like buying the food but I think they exaggerated that a bit. I wasn't there when she smoked pot in the lounge-room or when she made Ilana watch TV in your room. I believe that could have happened because Jodie could be a bitch at times. I know she wouldn't wash Ilana's clothes. I didn't see her smoking pot in the car, either. If I had seen that I would have been shocked but I don't think she would have done anything like that if I'd been there. You see I think she saw me as her ally, and perhaps I was, so she wouldn't have done anything to antagonize me.

'It was such an eventful time. Grandpa had been such a big part of our lives and losing him was a devastation. It happened so quickly that I couldn't believe it. I felt sorry for him, especially remembering those last couple of months which were so very sad. And I felt guilty, in a way, because I don't think I ever expressed myself properly to him. Do you remember when he gave us those gold pens? He wanted Aaron and me to have them because he thought he'd given too many things to Mark and not enough to us. I felt really sorry that he could think that he hadn't succeeded with us; so sad that he had to put things on such a materialistic level. That's why I felt guilty when he died because I don't think I ever made clear to him just what he had given to me. I mean, it wasn't a matter of possessions. What he gave me was a way of thinking. We used to spend so much time with him. I think I'd be a different person without the relationship we had with him and Grandma. He showed me what kindness is. He showed me what generosity is. I think I learned a lot morally and there was that degree of discipline that was lacking at home. They were more traditional; they didn't like swearing, and those attitudes helped to give a more balanced view of life. They were keen on aims and goals. They believed that people should be successful and they gave us something to strive for, a wish to be like them in some ways. I used to say to myself, I hope I'll be half as good a grandpa as he is.

'Every time I saw him, I learned something. Just his whole manner, the way he acted. His actions really did speak louder than his words. He was kind to everyone. Everyone was welcome. Everyone was beautiful. If I had a friend come over, that friend would be just like a grandson for the whole day. I really admired that. He was always wanting to help, always there.

'His death, just before you went away, really affected everything that happened here because, you see, Aaron and Ilana and I were so close to him. For example, I think his death would have made Ilana more ready to fight with Jodie. She had lost Grandpa and so, when things started to go wrong with Jodie, she was more ready to be upset and hurt. And Aaron,

77

you see, because of Grandpa's death, felt a much stronger sense of family obligation. You were away and Mark was away so he was the oldest person in the family and I think he wanted to be the father figure, the mature person here, the one keeping things in control. When he sensed something going wrong for one of us, he jumped in and fought for Ilana.

'Joseph was another thing in our lives that was changing. It was very disturbing for us to see someone whom we had known and trusted turning into something else, losing control of himself. So you see, everything was changing and everything we had known and trusted was falling apart. It was like dominoes falling down. One thing just lead to another.

'I've been thinking about Marcel and how he and I were thrown together during that time. I felt sorry for him throughout this episode. He was trying to bring himself into our family as another brother and it wasn't working. Nevertheless, he and I had a great time when we were by ourselves. He was someone for me to look up to, someone to replace all those other people whom I normally look up to.

'I probably look at all this differently from the others because the only things that happened to me were inside myself. I was not in conflict with other people. I just watched and locked away what I saw and it's only now that it's starting to make sense.

'I was shocked at the way Aaron and Ilana turned so bitterly against Jodie. They seemed to forget all the nice things that she had done for us. Certainly she had some bad qualities and some difficult problems, but she had some top qualities as well. She was a wonderful person to us for all those years. You can't love everything about anyone. She was still being friendly to me; she was still offering me good, sensible advice. I could see her faults but they were not so great that I could hate her. I realized how easy it is for people to turn around and hate another person. You can't just hate a person for some wrong they do you; you have to weigh that up against their good qualities. I think that's the main thing I learned from Grandpa. I'm sure he saw the bad side of people very clearly but he wasn't going to let that affect his liking of a person. He looked for the good in everyone.

'The others might complain about what happened while you were away in Nepal, but they shouldn't. It was a learning experience. It was beneficial. My only regret is that Jodie no longer has a place in our lives.'

'Maybe we will see her again,' said Sophie.

'I don't think so. Aaron and Ilana still feel so bitter about her.'

'You could go and see her, Paul, if you felt like it,' suggested Sophie. 'I'm sure she still lives at Manly.'

'No, I don't think so,' replied Paul. 'The more I think about it, the more I realize how much she did hurt Ilana. I'll just wait and see what happens.'

The next time Sophie and Ilana were alone at home Ilana said she was ready to tell her story. She did, however, lay down certain conditions. 'Now, Mum,' she said, 'you are not to interrupt me. You have to let me tell it exactly how I want to and please, don't look at me. Go over there. Sit in that beanbag and look out of the window. I'll sit over here where you can't see me.'

'Right,' said Sophie, turning away so that Ilana would not see her smile. After all, this was a serious matter.

'From the moment you stepped onto that plane,' Ilana began, 'everything changed. I remember asking Jodie a question. I said, "What are we going to do now?" and she answered me really spitefully. I thought to myself, that's a bit weird. I can't remember exactly how long I stayed at home after you left for Nepal. It couldn't have been more than a week and a half; then I stayed at Christine's for two weeks. After that I had to stay at Manly with Jodie while the boys were away with Dad.

'Heaps of things happened but the really bad things occurred mainly during that week that I stayed in her flat. The first night there was good fun. You know Jodie's friend Clare … well her two daughters were staying there as well. Jane and Lucy. Lucy's about my age, a bit younger, but we got on well together. But the next day things started to go wrong. We were in the super-market at Warringah Mall and Jodie was reading the stars in the newspaper while we were doing the shopping. I said, "Read Cancer." Jane and I were both Cancers. It said something about it being useless for a Cancer person to explain anything to another person because things would go wrong anyway and no one would listen to the explanation. I was trying to explain to Jodie that what it said in the stars didn't necessarily apply to all Cancerians.

'Jodie wouldn't let me talk. She said, "No, Ilana, I'm sorry but you're not meant to explain anything. It says so in your stars and so you'd better keep quiet, hadn't you?" and she walked off and I said, "You fucking bitch!" and I started telling her off, right in the middle of the supermarket. She was being so horrible to me and every time I tried to say anything she'd turn on me and say, "No, Ilana, it says in your stars that you're not meant to say anything." She was making sure that the prediction in the stars came true for me.

'The last day of my week at Manly, we went into a restaurant on the Corso. I said I wanted a pancake and then Jane and Lucy wanted pancakes as well and Jodie was furious with me. "Look what you've done now, Ilana. You've got everyone to order pancakes and I can't afford it." So I said, "I'll pay for my pancakes," because I had about thirty dollars of my own money. She paid for the others' pancakes and, what's more, she paid for them out of the money you'd give her for housekeeping. The same thing had kept happening all week. I kept having to pay for my own food and you were paying for those other two children. I couldn't really understand that, or, rather, I did work it out but it didn't make any sense to me. You'd given her money for us, not for strangers; here I was paying for myself and you were paying for them. It was the same thing with the car. You'd left her our car so that she could drive us around but she used it all the time. She never used her own car, even if she was doing something that was just for herself. So I wondered about all those things while we were waiting for our pancakes, but I felt I couldn't say anything about it.

'When the pancakes came, Jodie tried to show Jane how to eat properly with a knife and fork but she was holding Jane's hand in such an awkward way that it couldn't possibly work. So I said, "Look, Jodie, you're not doing it the right way because you can see she's not holding the knife properly," and she said, "Ilana, it's none of your business. I'm showing her how to do it, not you." Then I said, "But look! She's not holding it properly," and she got really spiteful and she said, "I didn't ask you, Ilana," and I said, "Fuck off, you bitch," really loudly, in the middle of the restaurant. She was so embarrassed. She got up and she walked out and I thought, oh, fuck.

'Fortunately, Aaron rang up that night and said, "We're back now. If Ilana wants to come home she can." Jodie got off the phone and I said, "Yes, yes, I want to go home." So we got into your Toyota and drove home. I remember getting out of the car. I had about five bags because I had all my clothes and roller skates and all the things I'd bought while I was staying at

Christine's house and I couldn't possibly carry all of them. She wouldn't help me; she just got out of the car and slammed the door. The boys came out and helped me and later I told them about all the awful things that had happened during that week.

'After we came back from Manly, she wouldn't wash my clothes. You can imagine how may clothes there were to wash. The boys had been away with Dad and I'd been away for almost three weeks. There was just the biggest mound of clothes imaginable. It was worse than anything you've ever seen. I think that our entire wardrobes, all combined, were piled up on the floor downstairs, waiting to be washed.

'At first I put my dirty clothes in my room but she got them and threw them down the stairs, picking some of them up on her way down. She separated my clothes from everyone else's and then she started the washing. I saw mine, still sitting in a separate pile and I thought, this is a bit queer. I could see what she was going to do. She wasn't going to wash my clothes at all. She was going to put them in the drier and pretend she'd washed them. And I thought, fuck, what's going on? This is a bit stupid. So I went and got my clothes and I told Aaron that she wouldn't wash them and he said, "Look, don't worry. I'll do them," and I said, "No, I want Mum to see that she's not looking after me properly. That's the only proof I've got," and he said, "Oh, well, it's up to you."

'So I took my clothes upstairs again and I put them on the floor outside the toilet and I thought, I'll just leave them there. I went away to do something else and when I came back I saw them thrown all over the stairs again. So I collected them again and Aaron said, "Don't worry. I'll wash them," so I let Aaron wash my clothes.

'When the clothes were all washed and dried, Jodie and Marcel sat downstairs in the playroom folding the clothes and sorting them into piles. I walked downstairs. I walked into the playroom … oh … I can't describe the tension that was in that room. There was a sort of electrical force of hate … I could feel all this hate coming from them. There was Marcel whom I hated so much and Jodie whom I hated so much. They'd done all the clothes so neatly. I wanted to run through all those neat piles and knock them all over. That would have felt really good. I didn't of course, but, oh, I wanted to ruin all their wonderful work.

'I hated the way they behaved that first week you were away. Flirting. Carrying on. Always touching each other. It was revolting. It was disgusting. It made me feel sick. That's why I had to go and stay at Christine's place. I had a lot of fun there. We went out a lot. We spent heaps of money. And it was good because, although we spent so much time together, we didn't start to hate each other. I couldn't have gone home. I couldn't have walked through that door. I intended to stay a Christine's house until the day you came back but then they kicked me out. They said I had to go so I had to ring Jodie up and I said, "Look, Jodie, Christine's family are going to kick me out. I've got nowhere to go." So she picked me up that night and we went home for an hour or so. I saw Joseph there and he and I had a bit of a laugh and then Jodie took me back with her to Manly for the week.

'Marcel was such a cunt that first week you were away. He really was. He made these statues out of clay. He made them over and over and they all looked the same. They looked like the Virgin Mary. I said to him, "That looks like fucking Mary, you stupid idiot," and he said, "It's not. It's just a woman." And

I said, "Well, how come you keep making them all the same?" and he said, "They're not all the same. They're all different in their own way."

'Jodie made this clay pot for Marcel. It was like a cup. About two weeks ago I saw it sitting on a shelf downstairs and I broke it. I broke it by throwing it on the floor. I said to Paul, "Fuck, man, I want to smash this!" and he said, "Okay then, smash it." So I smashed it and that made me feel really good and I took the pieces to school and I said to Marcel, "Here's your fucking pot, you bastard," and then I walked off. That's what I said to Marcel and although I do talk to him now, I won't forgive him, no way, because he's a conman. He used to flirt with me all the time and then he started flirting with Jodie. I can't forgive him for that.

'Jodie was meant to be my guardian, my female companion, but she turned out to be an enemy. I remember one day, on the beach, she said to me, "There's something wrong with you, Ilana, because you can't express sexual feelings at your age. You'll never be able to feel love." And this was on the beach! There were about five of her friends there. I mean, I'm only twelve years old. I don't think I'm ready to express sexual feelings yet. I just turned around to her and said, "Get fucked, Jodie," and I stood up and walked off. I told her to get fucked a few times, usually in public. I had to because she treated me like dirt.

'I don't know why she changed. I think she felt that, being my guardian, she had some kind of power over me but I wouldn't let her have that power.

'I don't know what I would have done without Christine. She was so understanding; she was like a mother to me. In that time I was at Christine's I didn't have a shower once, not until I went away with her family to Lake Macquarie for a few days where I nearly got killed in the shower. I was having a shower and I didn't know how to use the hot-water system. It was one of those really old-fashioned ones. I turned it off the wrong way and all this steam went through the house and it nearly blew up and Christine's father had to come and save me. I think that was one of the reasons why they kicked me out. He nearly had a heart attack. It was very funny but a bit scary. That was the first shower I had in two weeks. I didn't brush my teeth; I didn't wash my hair, but I don't think you could smell it on me. I lived on the floor. I slept on the floor. And I ate takeaway food every night. I had a really good time. We used to go out shopping every day. I bought all this make-up and records and clothes because Grandpa said, when he gave me that barmitzvah money, he said, "Spend it on whatever you want," and so I thought, oh, I'm really raging and I spent it all.

'What really gives me the shits is that, before any of this happened, Jodie and I were like sisters. Losing that closeness was really quite a tragedy. I remember thinking that it was all like a play and that perhaps it was not real. Perhaps I was just sitting and watching it. I was the poor innocent girl and Christine was the faithful friend; Joseph was the neurotic Portugese; Marcel was the Argentinian conman; Jodie was the American apple pie. I used to look at your portrait on the lounge-room wall and I knew you were watching over me.

'I didn't hate you for going away. That would have been stupid. I came to grips with the fact that you wanted to go on holidays, but I was angry, in a way, and then I realized, no, it's not your fault. You can't say, I shouldn't have gone, I shouldn't have left you, because perhaps Jodie would have betrayed us in some other way at some other time. Perhaps she might have done small things over a longer period of time that would have made us realise that she was not the person we thought her to be.

'I did grow up a lot. I learned about the different human emotions. I learned what real friends are. I learned about real people, whether they're genuine or not. Things like that. I think that what happened was inevitable and I think that we're lucky that it's behind us because it can't happen again. When you've seen once what can happen to people, then you'll be ready for it the next time.

'I remember the day you got back, I said, "Oh, Mum, give her a hundred dollars; she helped out so well." I think I said that because I wanted to pretend to myself that nothing bad had happened; it was just some sort of minor thing, nothing important. I can't believe I said that to you, "Oh, Mum, give her some more money for helping out so well." I actually said that. Ah ... fuck ... it makes you feel like a fool.

'Perhaps it wasn't her fault. Perhaps it was no-one's fault. Perhaps something happened to her that made her behave in that way; but I can't forgive her for taking out on me whatever it was that had happened to her. No-one has the right to do that to anyone. I've certainly learned about losing people. She's dead to me but perhaps she'll haunt me, like a ghost.

'While you were away I would imagine that you were the clouds and the moon and that Mark was the stars and you both used to watch over me and I could always think, oh, Mum will be home soon and all this will end, but I couldn't escape to you in a letter because I was scared you would think, oh, shit, I'll have to go back home and save my daughter from this terrible situation, but you were always there above me, like Karma, I suppose. It was a very painful time for me but I knew that, as soon as you got back, everything, everything would be alright.'

OASIS

I needed a man so I joined a 'friendship' club and put an advertisement in their newsletter. It seemed a reasonable thing to do. It's not easy to meet men. I don't meet potential lovers at my place of work. I used to meet men at nudist beaches but I've given up lying in the sun. It bores me. It's counter-productive. I don't go to pubs or clubs. I don't like drinking alcohol and talking all night. I'm a bit unsociable, I suppose. What I do like is making love so that's why I joined the friendship club.

This is the ad I put in:

> *WANTED – a man in his forties; good-humoured, tolerant, affectionate, sensual, intelligent.*
>
> *I AM – a teacher and writer, warm, sensuous, affectionate, intelligent, incurably honest and highly creative. Enjoy theatre, films, eating at cheap restaurants. Looking for a friend and lover forever.*

I signed the ad 'WRITER'. I didn't put anything about having four children. I thought that would frighten any man away.

When I looked through the ads other people had put in the newsletter, I didn't hold out much hope. Men in their forties seemed to be looking for women in their thirties and I felt angry about that. In fact, I felt angry about the whole business of having to look for a lover. When Michael lived with me I didn't have to look for anything. It was all provided for me. He was the person I went out with; he was the person I snuggled up to at night; he was the person I made love to. I didn't have to worry about anything. Most of all, I didn't have to worry about being in my forties. Now I had to face the problem that maybe no-one would ever want to make love to me again. It was an awesome thought.

I received only one reply to my advertisement:

20 October 1983

I am in my fifties, WRITER, rather than my forties, but otherwise the specifications you mention for your future friend and lover would seem to cover my own attributes.

You'll never know for sure, however, unless you drop me a line and permit a certain amount of communication to go on for a while.

Perhaps you'd like to tell me more about yourself. Perhaps you'd like a ring, a personal visit, a date in some public spot, a lift from a street corner?

Your abilities would appear to be rather formidable at first glance. Could anyone at all live up to such a blurb?

Sincerely,

JOHN

He had a Neutral Bay address on the letter, but no telephone number. I was glad of that because it gave me the opportunity to write about myself, rather than to talk about myself. I didn't like his use of the word 'blurb'. It seemed like a slur on my list of attributes. I thought I'd described myself with reasonable accuracy.

I wrote back to him. I told him all about myself, about my teaching, my writing, my kids. I told him I wasn't looking for a father for my children; in fact I wanted a relationship that would provide me with a respite from my domestic responsibilities. I thought it was safer to say that. And I took him to task for his implied criticism in the use of the word 'blurb'. Was it so strange, I asked him, that I had actually succeeded in writing two novels? He sent a swift reply.

27 October 1983

No, it's not so strange, SOPHIE, that you should have succeeded in the most difficult creative field of them all. Wasn't it Bertrand Russell who pointed out that the writing of a novel was the most complex mental exercise in the universe? Anyway, your letter provides plenty of evidence of your capabilities (meticulous forming of the letters, broad vocabulary to select from, maximum meaning conveyed with minimum effort for the reader, implications moving in a shadowy fashion behind the foreground declarations).

The idea of kids in the background is, to me, disturbing. All my bachelor habits have been formed without the need to cater for growing youngsters.

Lazy hours of sexual enjoyment are a constant objective in the back of my mind, even when I'm working for a living, which is rather rare these days. Fifteen years ago I was an alcoholic, so I shy away from that pastime these days.

This weekend I have to try to get up to Canberra but I'll be back about next Tuesday. You might drop me a note suggesting a tentative meeting. If you are home during the day I could slip out and see you.

JOHN

I wrote back and explained that my house was impossible as a meeting place. In my house, there is a great deal of love but absolutely no privacy. It is impossible for any of us to go anywhere without the rest of us wanting and expecting to know exactly what is going on. So I suggested that, under the circumstances, it would be better if I called on him.

1 November 1983

Pop over next Friday afternoon, SOPHIE, as soon as you've finished teaching. I'll give you cod mornay and cheap champagne with a lot of frantic chitchat.

The block of flats, 'Kingston', is on the corner of Royal and McDougall Streets, if you'd care to peruse your Gregory's.

Come up to the fourth floor and don't knock on door E: it will be unlocked. Come right in.

Bon courage,

JOHN

I certainly needed courage. I wrote back and said how awful it was for people to have to engage in 'frantic chitchat.' I, myself, I told him, was an absolutely compulsive talker when I first met anyone. I needed to keep talking to fill in the spaces of possible silences and to hide my shyness. I was, I told him, afraid of meeting people for the first time. Wouldn't it be marvellous, I wrote, if people could get to know each other by osmosis, instead of having to resort to chitchat.

3 November 1983

Osmosis first, SOPHIE, verbal intercourse as a last resort. As soon as you surmount your misgivings sufficiently to open that door and step into the apartment, then proceed to the bathroom. No need for words. After a long day at Tech, you will want to soak in a tepid bath or shower away all that fatigue. Fresh towels ready awaiting.

> This could be a good idea. I'll need time to coax a
> meal into being while you are adapting yourself
> to the local habitat. If you want champagne
> before the bath, just look expectantly as you
> breeze by.
>
> Listen, did you know that dandelions are
> members of a true single-parent family? They
> are indeed clones of one another since dandelions
> are apomictic.
>
> JOHN

I had to look up 'apomictic' in the dictionary and I decided, then and there, that I wanted to make love to any man who could use words that I had to look up in a dictionary.

I approached our meeting with a mixture of excitement and trepidation. What if he were monstrous? What if he had two heads? What if he were a rapist? What if he were a murderer? No-one knew where I was going. What if I disappeared and no-one ever found me? And what would I say when I walked in? Would I maintain silence, as he had suggested, and just drift into his bathroom and take a shower? Impossible! Hot and sticky though I felt, I could not imagine myself doing that. I was wearing a pink and white Indian skirt and a pale pink silk blouse. I felt quite attractive, really.

I found his block of units and parked my car. I wanted to turn around and drive back home but I decided to be brave. I got into the lift and went up to the fourth floor. The door was unlocked as he had told me it would be and I turned the knob and opened the door and walked in. It was cool and quiet inside his apartment. He was sitting in an armchair facing the door when I arrived. He uncurled himself and stood up, somewhat cautiously, as I came into the room. He was tall and slim with very short, graying hair, slightly bald.

'My goodness me, Sophie,' he said, 'you were courageous, weren't you? I didn't think you'd come. Do you want a bath?'

'No, no,' I replied.

'Sit down here, then, and I'll pour you a nice glass of champagne. Now you just sit there and sip your champagne and get used to the place while I do something about dinner. I'm a terrible cook, you know. I don't know the first thing about cooking.'

In less than five minutes he had drawn up a small, portable table between our two armchairs and put before me a plate containing a piece of smoked cod and a pile of hot chips, the frozen packet kind, crinkle-cut.

'I was going to make a cheese sauce to go over the fish but, quite honestly, I don't know how to do it. Is it alright? Will it do? If it's very terrible I could go over and get some Chinese takeaway. You see, I didn't really think you'd come. Let me pour you some more champagne.'

'Aren't you going to have some champagne?' I asked.

'No, no, not for me. I told you I used to be an alcoholic. These days, if I go anywhere, I just hold a glass of beer in my hand but I never drink it.'

'I don't need alcohol, you know. I could go for the rest of my life without ever having another drink,' I assured him.

'That's good, that's very good. If you ever decide to visit me again, I'll give you apple cider to drink. Or pineapple juice. Do you like pineapple juice? I just thought champagne was the right thing to do.'

'I'm not really very hungry,' I said, toying with my thick fillet of cod. I've been a bit nervous, you know, about coming here.'

'That's just what I've been thinking,' said John. 'That's why I decided you mightn't come. After all, how could you know what I'm like?'

'Yes,' I said. 'You might have been a rapist or a murderer or a pervert. How could I know?'

'I'm not, you know, I'm not any of those things. Do you know what I thought? I thought you'd be large and middle-aged and frumpy. I thought if you were a teacher and a writer you'd be serious and stern. And look at you! So little! Such a beautiful girl! I can't believe it, really I can't. Have some more champagne.'

'No. I don't want any more, thank you.'

'Would you like to listen to some music?' John asked. 'I've only got two records. They're both Chopin. I don't know anything about music, really, but someone left them here. So I play them sometimes. Would you like to listen to them?'

I nodded.

'Come in here, then, and lie down on the bed with me and I'll put them on.'

I lay down and he lay down beside me and I let him put his arm under my head. He didn't try to kiss me. I lay there for five minutes and then I said, 'Well, if we're going to make love I want to have a shower first.'

'Sophie, we don't have to make love, you know,' said John. 'I'm just glad you came. I'm just pleased to know you.'

'I think we'd better make love,' I said. 'I came here to make love. Before I came I decided that I wanted to make love to the man who sent me those letters.'

I went into the bathroom. He followed me. 'Here, I'll just show you how this shower works.'

'I'll be right.'

93

'You can use this brown towel. It's fresh and clean. Now don't slip when you're getting out of the bathtub. I don't know what we'd do if you had a fall.'

'I'll be right, really,' I said, waiting for him to go. He left the bathroom and closed the door. I stood under the shower for a long time. It was still light. A long summer evening light. I felt detached. I felt alienated. It was as if I were watching myself instead of being inside myself. I was very nervous. It was six months since Michael had left me and no man had touched me in all that time. Celibacy. Sweet self-containment. Satisfaction, of a kind. As I stood under the shower tears for Michael mingled with the water. I turned off the shower and rubbed myself dry. I opened the bathroom door and went into the bedroom. He was lying naked on the bed. I lay down beside him. He kissed me and I felt nothing – no passion, no excitement – nothing. 'Look,' I said, 'I've been celibate for six months. I've become a virgin again.'

'That's alright,' he said. 'That's quite alright. You stay a virgin. Lie down now. Just lie down. You don't have to do anything.'

I lay back and closed my eyes. He ran his hands over my body. 'My, what a beautiful girl you are,' he said. 'You're like one of those marvellous Rubens paintings.'

'I'm going to Nepal in six weeks' time,' I said. 'I'm going trekking in the Himalayas.'

'Are you really? You do make the most of life, don't you? My goodness me, how do you manage everything? Teaching, writing, looking after your children and now trekking in Nepal. I can see how fit you are. Very healthy skin. Firm flesh. Oh yes, you'll do very well in Nepal. Very well indeed.'

He continued to stroke my body, gently, patiently. He stroked my arms, my breasts, my belly, my thighs. 'Now, Sophie, you

OASIS

just leave this to me. I know exactly what you need. You lie
there and relax. You don't have to do a thing. I'll just get you
a little vaseline.'

I lay on my back with my eyes closed, my arms spread wide
across the bed, my legs parted. He sat beside me, with his back
to me and he began to massage my clitoris with a generous
supply of vaseline.

'Now, Sophie, there's no hurry. You just enjoy yourself. This
should take as long as possible, you know. Oh, you're very well
made. What a beautiful girl!' He mesmerized me with his gentle,
teasing touch. I felt as if I were floating out to sea on lulling
waves that rose and fell, carrying me higher and higher and
further and further away from myself. As he sensed my rising
heat, he bent over me and began to use both hands, one gently
caressing my clitoris, the other between my legs, fingers everywhere – in my cunt, up my arse. His arm became a giant penis
thundering home and he brought me to a single shattering
orgasm and as I came, tears fell from my eyes. 'Oh, darling,' he
murmured, 'darling Sophie, how wonderful you are.' He held
me in his arms, 'Now, wasn't that good? We did very well, don't
you think? You had a beautiful orgasm.'

'One orgasm's no good to me,' I cried. 'I need twenty.' He
must have thought I was mad. 'My father's dying. There's death
all around me,' I sobbed and he just held on to me until I'd
finished. Then I stopped crying. 'I'm alright now,' I said, sniffing.

'Next time you come I'll give you a wonderful massage, from
head to toe. How would you like that?'

'Yes,' I replied, 'yes, yes. I'd love that.'

He got out of bed, quite suddenly and put on his clothes.
'Well, Sophie, it's nine o'clock. You've had a big day. I think it's

time you got dressed and got in your car and drove home. You need a good sleep.' I got up and hastily dressed.

'But what about you? I've done nothing to satisfy your sexuality.'

'Oh, don't you worry about me. You've given me quite enough.'

'But you haven't had an orgasm. That doesn't seem fair,' I said.

'That's not important. Come on now. Off home to bed. Now, when are we going to see you again?'

'How about Tuesday morning?' I suggested.

'Good, good. Now you take it easy. Don't drive too fast and get plenty of rest. You need your rest you know. Goodness me, the busy life you lead. You certainly need plenty of rest.' And he bundled me out of the door. I didn't know what to make of him.

I felt strangely depressed when I got home. I don't know why. I was so depressed that I ate three bread rolls, a packet of chocolate biscuits and two plates of ice-cream with chocolate sauce. That made me even more depressed. And then I wrote him a letter. I told him that he was a nice man and that I liked him but that I felt miserable and that, whenever I got miserable, I became a compulsive eater. I tried to explain about the compulsion to eat, as if he were some kind of therapist who might be able to understand. I let the whole of myself flow onto the pages. I told him that it was strange to be with any man except Michael. I told him how hurt I had been when Michael left me. I told him how exhausted I felt at the thought of having to start again with someone else. I told him how difficult life was. I told him how awful it was to have a mother with Alzheimer's disease. I told him how terrible it was to watch my father disintegrate and stumble towards death. I went on and on and on and then I sealed the letter in an envelope and dashed up to the post office and put it in the box. The minute I posted the letter I wanted to bash down the post box and retrieve it. I went home more miserable than ever. I was sure I'd never hear from him again. I got a letter in the post on Monday.

4 November 1983

Superb SOPHIE,

The best chocolate biscuits are Newport, so good that they have to be avoided.

Tuesday ten-thirty, you get tea and biscuits. At noon, if required, the Chinese takeaway goes into action. Meanwhile quietly controlled excitement building to a climax.

What prevents your crumbling under formidable burdens is the knowledge that, by any standard, your daily performance would exhilarate anyone. What knocks others down into depression is not the overwhelming effort of tackling gigantic problems, but the admission within themselves that they have nothing to be proud of.

Don't train too hard for Nepal. Your silky skin indicates excellent health right now. All you have to do is maintain that condition and you can face anything. A brisk mile walk takes about fifteen minutes; so now and again this is all you need to allay deterioration.

JOHN

When I received this letter I cried and then I smiled. I felt greatly relieved. I could pour out my heart to him and he was not going to run away. I needed an audience and I needed intimacy. It was not sex that I missed. What I had missed over the last six months was cuddling and comfort and the intimacy of whispered words. Yes, I decided that John would definitely do.

When I arrived at 4E Kingston the following day, he welcomed me with a kiss of such passionate intensity that I felt almost humbled by it.

'Would you like some tea?' he asked, between kisses.

'No, no,' I replied, 'I want to make love.'

'That's good. Very good indeed. Now there's a towel on the bed. You just take off your clothes and lie on your stomach. I'm going to give you a nice massage.' He got out a bottle of polyunsaturated vegetable oil. I was a bit horrified but he assured me that vegetable oil was quite odourless and very effective as a massage oil. He began with my toes, then the soles of my feet, my ankles, then my calves, my knees, my thighs. He was a vigorous and expert masseur and I was quite surprised. I thought that the massage, like the Chopin, was going to be nothing more than a tool of seduction. Then he sat on my legs and gave my bottom and back and neck a thorough going over. I was sorry when he stopped. I liked the feel of his weight and the touch of his skin.

'Now roll over and I'll do the front,' he said.

'You're pretty good at this,' I said. 'You must have had a lot of practice.'

'Ah, well,' he replied, 'one picks up these little things.'

'Who taught you?' I asked.

''Oh, goodness me, I can't remember things like that,' he laughed.

'Tell me how old you are,' I asked.

'I'm one hundred and eight,' he replied. 'Now just close your eyes and drift off while I finish this massage. No talking now.' So I let myself sink into the bed. Now he allowed the massage to become sensuous, touching, stroking, teasing until I thought I would explode. He made me wait, knowing exactly how to excite me, how to bring me to a level of exquisite desire, how to retreat and calm, how to build again to unbearable passion until orgasm after orgasm burst from my body. His hand was relentless and my vagina felt on fire as he conjured spasm after spasm from my willing flesh. In the end I had to stop him.

'No more,' I cried, 'I can't stand any more,' and my body was shaking and my hands were trembling and he covered me with kisses and I hugged him and kissed him and threw my arms around him and tears sprang out of my eyes and flooded my face.

'There now,' he said, 'you've had your twenty orgasms. Now what you need is a nice cup of tea. Bushell's Blue Label. You just lie there now. I'll be back in a jiffy,' and he covered me with a sheet and patted my head. He put a towel around his waist and went into the kitchen. He was back in a few minutes with a traymobile laden with tea, milk, fruit, cheese, nuts, rice wafers. He put two pillows behind me and sat me up. He put a tea-towel over my lap and gave me a plate for my food. He cut up the cheese and peeled apples and poured the tea. He wouldn't let me do anything.

'The other night, when I came here, why didn't you do anything to satisfy your own sexuality?' I asked.

'I wanted to be sure you'd come back,' he replied. 'Now, when are we going to see you again?'

'How about Friday?' I said.

'Good. Very good. Now eat up, Sophie. Do you want some more tea? How about a few nuts?'

'No, I've had enough,' I replied. 'I try not to eat too much in the middle of the day.'

He put Chopin on the record player. 'Now you lie down and relax while I see to these dishes.' I lay down and gazed around the room. I could hear him in the kitchen, washing up the dishes. Everything in the apartment was so neat. The rooms looked unlived-in. He had bookshelves in the lounge room but they were bare except for telephone books. There were no paintings on the walls; there were no possessions scattered around. It seemed strange to me.

He came back and got into bed with me. 'Now what you need is a nice sleep,' he said. I curled into his arms and rested my head on his chest.

'It's very peaceful here,' I said.

'That's why I bought it. This place is like an oasis. A little haven of sanity in a desert of madness. That's just what you need in your life, Sophie, now isn't it?'

I sighed and snuggled further into his arms. I breathed in the odour of his skin. My hand touched the soft flesh of his buttocks. His skin was smooth and almost hairless, velvet to the touch. I put my hand on his penis and felt it swell in my palm. He put his hand between my legs and gently stroked my clitoris. We lay there for a long time, tingling, tender, gentle, sensuous. Then I slid down the bed and cradled his testicles in my hand and let my tongue play with his penis. I ran my tongue slowly up and down the length of his penis and took the tip into my mouth and he lay there, luxuriating; his turn to be attended to. Then, quite suddenly, he got up. He went into the bathroom and came back with the jar of vaseline. He spread it quite liberally over my clitoris, the entrance to my vagina, my anus and then he lay down on his back and positioned me on top of him. My breasts rested on his belly, my clitoris lay on his chest, my mouth was free to continue paying lascivious attention to his penis. He positioned his hands so that his fingers seemed to be everywhere inside me, filling all my cavities, his thumb never leaving my clitoris. We moved so slowly, so imperceptibly that we seemed to be suspended in stillness, hushed in a silence that was broken only by the heat of our breaths, fanning each other. It was exquisite. It was ecstasy. I wanted the moment to last forever. The movement gradually increased, building, mounting until I could hold back no longer and I thrust myself against him in violent orgasm. He slid from under me and entered me from behind. He entered, withdrew, entered, withdrew, teasing himself. The he pulled me up onto my knees and I could feel the whole of my back against his chest and belly and he put his hands on my breasts and held me there. I put my head back so that his face pressed against mine. I did not feel human. I felt like a wolf, wild and howling, coupling in the wind. And then he came inside me, with powerful, vigorous strokes, hot and fierce. Then he manoeuvred me onto my side and lay there, curled around me, his penis still inside me, throbbing, pulsating coming endlessly. We did not move. We did not speak. He nuzzled his nose into my shoulder. I felt as if all my chromosomes had been rearranged. He got up very suddenly, before I was ready to let him go.

'Now, what you need is a nice cup of tea and a tepid bath before you go home,' he said and dashed into the kitchen, as if nothing extraordinary had happened at all.

He brought back the tea. Sipping from my cup I said to him, 'Look, could we talk about this?'

'Oh, my goodness me, no. Talking doesn't do any good. You write me a nice letter, that's much the best way. Now drink your tea. We do very well, you know, very well indeed.'

So I kept quiet about what had happened in the bed. I drank my tea and I had a shower and I went and picked the kids up from school. I cooked the dinner and talked to the children and then I went over to see my father and mother. I did all these things in a robot-like fashion. John clung to me like an aura. I could feel his presence all over me. When I got home that night, I wrote him a letter and dashed up to the post office with it. How, I asked him, had he managed to conjure up such powerful orgasms from my body? How was I going to live until next Friday? Was it as wondrous for him as it was for me? I raved on and on. I got a letter back on Thursday. I was amazed at the efficiency of Australia Post. If I posted a letter one evening, he actually received it the next day.

9 November 1983

Your novel, SOPHIE, has been in and out of the library. I've been trying to borrow it.

'But I reserved it.'

'So did the person who's got it now. Your turn will come.'

For each of us, no doubt, our turn will come to slip across that Stygian creek, that pit of Acheron. That is why waiting is a criminal waste of time. We must cram as much as possible into life while the cramming is available. For goodness' sake, go easy in Nepal. I hear that the tracks are rugged and treacherous north-west of Kathmandu.

Discretion and restraint will need to be our motto if languorous hours are to stretch into the remote future. Surrounding me are various cronies and relations, some of whom would regard a sexual affair as a punishable offence. I treat such persons as friends but of course, in my heart, I am not misled by the apparent benevolence of their attitudes.

Next Friday evening you will receive Bushell's Blue Label plus cold chicken and a lettuce leaf. Perhaps a round, ripe pear and crisp brown nuts.

Of course you always run the risk of finding
yourself on the menu.

JOHN

This letter puzzled me. It seemed to have nothing to do
with the letter I had written to him. 'Discretion' and 'restraint'
– what did he mean? I'd never been discrete and restraint was
something I knew nothing about.

On Friday I charged in, ready to confront him. 'What do
you mean by "discretion"? Are you ashamed of being my lover?
Won't you go out with me? Do I have to keep our affair a
secret? What do you mean?'

He took hold of me and sat down in his armchair. He pulled
me down onto his lap and gently pushed my head into his neck
and hugged me. 'Now, Sophie, I'm an old bachelor, set in my
ways. You will have to understand that. You will have to be my
secret. That's the only way.'

'But that's hypocritical,' I cried, sitting up straight and push-
ing his arms away.

'We're all hypocrites, Sophie. In fact, hypocrisy is one of
my guiding lights. It's the only way to protect yourself in a
double-dealing world. Hypocrisy and discretion and restraint.
If you over-indulge yourself in a sexual relationship, it doesn't
last. If you exercise restraint, it can go on forever.'

'I'm not a hypocrite,' I replied. 'I'm a totally honest person
and I'm trying to tell you that I don't think a relationship can
be conducted in your way.'

'Now tell me, Sophie, what did you have for breakfast
this morning?'

'I'm trying to say something to you!' I declared, loudly. I
looked at him. I could see that he was not going to participate

in a confrontation. 'Actually, I had yoghurt and fruit with bran sprinkled on the top.'

'That's a very healthy breakfast. Now why don't you take off your clothes and lie down on the towel on the bed and I'll give you a lovely massage.'

I wrote him a letter when I got home, about truth and honesty and lack of hypocrisy. I told him those were my guiding lights. I told him that I did not know how to be a hypocrite and that I was certainly lacking in restraint. I told him that I was the kind of person who jumped into rivers, headlong, without testing the depth, without knowing whether I'd sink or swim.

15 November 1983

I finally got a copy of your novel from the library, SOPHIE. Their copy looks as though it has been through a chaff cutter, even though they have gummed hard covers on it. What makes your novel a success, SOPHIE, is the plain truth. Not many people can deal with unmodified truth, especially in matters concerning their own track records. It has been said that what differentiates humans most from animals is our ability, eagerness even, to distort the record in order to spare our own feelings.

Your novel offers the reader insight, often with startling impact, into a real individual dealing with genuine problems in an authentic world. A cautionary tale for those contemplating life's journey; and mesmeric reading for anyone who recognizes the pathway but has never seen it expressed in words before.

What's all this about jumping into rivers headlong? The main danger about rivers is shallowness. Broken bones are the risk you run in trying to cross torrents. This is why it pays to seek out deep places for passing over to the other side.

Such a torrent of inventiveness and yearning
for insight must give rise to expression on
your part. That is why you write. One theory is
that all of literature is merely a manifestation
of displacement activity, like adjusting your
clothing when you feel nervous. Well, when you
feel nervous, you've just got to let the welling
waves wash over the brim a little and arrange
the stranded ideas neatly on foolscap for your
publisher's perusal.

I've never met a serious person before. I've
certainly never known anyone who was in
relentless pursuit of the truth.

See you on Friday.

JOHN

I would lie in his arms, after lovemaking, and he would say,
'Now I'll tell you the story of my life.' Then he would recount
some anecdote from his past, a story about Africa or Denmark
or the Persian Gulf. Most of his life had been spent working overseas for the United Nations. His stories were always
amusing, informative and interesting but decidedly lacking in
the revelation of self. At the end of his story he would say, 'Oh,
you do make me prattle on. No-one else does that. You must
be terribly bored.'

'Why didn't you ever marry?' I asked.

'I nearly did once, you know,' he replied, 'but the lady I was
going to marry, who was a member of the Danish Diplomatic
Service, found out she'd lose all her superannuation if we married, so we gave up on the idea.'

He never said he loved me. In fact, he made sure that I
understood that he had absolutely no feelings. He told me that
his life experience had been such that it had left him incapable
of feeling. 'I'm an observer,' he said, 'detached from life, sitting

on the sidelines, watching the game. I'm like the boards on which the players walk. I'll tell you something, though. People say that you can never run away from yourself or your own problems but my life is an absolute proof that this isn't true. If anything disturbs me I just pack up and live somewhere else for a year or two.'

'The thing I admire most about you,' I said, 'is that you're so independent. You don't seem to need anyone.'

'We all need other people, Sophie. No-one is independent,' he replied. 'I'll tell you what,' he said, hugging me, 'this could be dangerous. I could get too fond of you.'

'Will you send me away if you get too fond of me?' I asked.

'Oh, dear me, no!'

I kissed him passionately. I could not kiss him enough.

'Now look here,' he said, 'are you ever coming back?'

'Of course I'm coming back,' I replied.

'What would I ever do without you, Sophie?'

In my next letter I told him that he'd better watch it. Fond-ness could be dangerous for a man with no feelings. I told him everything in my letters. All my thoughts, all my feelings, all my sorrow, all my fears. I told him that sometimes I thought I might be insane. I told him that I thought the world was going to be destroyed any minute. I told him that what mattered most was that I should fulfil my potential as quickly as possible, before I was blown to bits by a nuclear blast. I told him how much I felt an obligation to my European Jewish past, that I must strive and succeed and carry on my genetic line.

26 November 1983

You have certainly never seemed insane to me, SOPHIE. Quite the contrary. Wholesome and forward-looking would be a more apt description, rather than unsound and fixated.

'Fiddler on the Roof', even the Talmud, SOPHIE, doesn't go back nearly far enough. There were forces in concert millions of years ago which eventually succeeded in giving rise to your unique blend of individuality. Thank goodness.

Now you feel that catastrophe looms imminently to wipe away all trace of your emergence from existence in the millions of years that lie ahead. In all likelihood you are right. As Toynbee said: 'Never before have people failed to use the weapons at their disposal, and never before have the weapons been so edged.'

Let us be of good heart, despite the threat of doom; keeping in mind that far more improbable odds have already been overcome in the long process that produced yourself. Go back even twenty or thirty generations and the chances of those myriads of ancestors all cooperating in exactly the right moment to culminate in SOPHIE are unbelievably slim.

On Friday, towards sundown, you will get a chicken together with some other healthy foodstuff and lots of attention to your silky skin.

JOHN

My letters were full of emotion, passion, longing, desire. His were always controlled, wise, calm. His passion was entirely contracted into the hours of our togetherness. He depressed me in a way, because I wanted my lover to be an integrated part of my life and he insisted on remaining only a strand of my existence.

'Tell me,' I asked, 'what it was like when you were young.'

'Goodness me, Sophie, I thought you realised I was never young. I was born old. I'll tell you something, though, you're

107

just the right temperature, just the right taste. Oh, you are a comfort!'

'What kind of things are you afraid of?' I wanted to know. 'I'm afraid of natural disasters; storms at sea, lightening, thunder, heavy rain. Are you afraid of those things?'

'No, not at all,' he replied.

'What then?' I insisted. 'What are you afraid of?'

'I'm afraid of women,' he laughed.

'Really? Are you afraid of me?'

'I'm absolutely terrified of you, Sophie.' I hugged him, close and tight. Despite all the defences he put up to keep me from knowing him, I knew that he meant what he had just said.

I talked this relationship over with a friend of mine and she said I was mad to put up with this situation. A relationship with a man meant going out, not just going to bed. I was being used, my friend insisted. He ought to go to restaurants with me, to the theatre, to movies. He ought to be prepared to meet the kids.

I asked him to go to the theatre with me. I begged him. I even bought tickets. I bought them for a Friday night, a night I usually spent with him anyway. I thought he might come but on the Thursday I received a letter from him.

7 December 1983

Friday, SOPHIE, becomes impossible. My niece is having a birthday party for her son and I am expected to attend. I leave for an extended visit to Canberra on Saturday and won't be back before 20 December.

JOHN

I did not understand why he was incapable of what I considered to be a normal relationship but I understood that it was not caused by unwillingness. For some reason it was impossible for him to go out with me so I decided not to expect of him any more than he was capable of giving. After all, if a simple request to accompany me to the theatre could result in a ten day absence, then I'd be a fool to try the same sort of thing again. He was an enigma to me but I knew, with absolute certainly, that all the feeling he denied in himself he allowed to be expressed in the sexual act, and because of that he brought to lovemaking an intensity of passion that I found irresistible.

My father died while John was away and his absence made me furious. I needed warmth. I needed comfort. I needed my retreat to his oasis. I wrote him an angry letter telling that I hated him for going away just when I needed him.

20 December 1983

You will find the world tinged with sadness for a while, SOPHIE, even though you feel a certain release. This is the moment for an emotional retreat. Let the world go by without too much struggle from yourself for the time being. Don't hurry the processes of recovery, yet rest assured that recover you shall; soon to take up the themes of your lives once more.

Come over in the next few days if you have time. You must be busy getting ready for your adventure in Nepal.

My arms are about you.

JOHN

Our last lovemaking was as satisfactory as usual and we arranged to meet a month later, on 27 January, at 5 pm. When

I arrived in Kathmandu there was a letter from him waiting for me.

21 December 1983

Don't say you've forgotten your notebook and
felt-tip pen, SOPHIE. What you have to bring
back from the loftiest landscape on earth are
not Buddhas carved in green limestone and
betel nuts but fresh, on-the-spot observations
together with first-hand notes of conversations
going on about you. For a writer contemplating
an attack upon another book, there is no better
ammunition than this.

Try to write things down as they occur, even
sketchily. Ideas go bad if left in the memory
and emerge after an interval devoid of their
original sharpness having suffered a sea-change.
Processes of the mind work to reduce ideas
to uninspiring conformity. You must strive to
avoid this.

It is almost impossible to record others'
conversations directly without capturing the
irony that fascinates readers. Apparently
Sigmund Freud said that intellect was what
people used to explain the actions their instincts
pushed them to perform. Almost every utterance
contains inadvertent rationalisation; the speaker
offering socially acceptable motives for behaviour
over which there was little or no control anyway.

So get to work. Not easy, as any journalist will
tell you, for all your daily quantum of energy is
taken up in merely surviving. But to be a writer,
you have to be at least two hundred percent
efficient. Not an impossible proposition for the
multi-lived SOPHIE.

Avoid the usual hazards. Watch out for weevils
in the flour, buffaloes in the ghee, cockroaches
in the teapot, scorpions on the shower curtain,
rabid royal tigers in the undergrowth, Gurkhas

in the gharries. Above all, keep your distance
from the anopheles mosquito on the outskirts of
Kathmandu; more dangerous than the Chitwan
elephant or rhinoceros.

Don't neglect to have a detailed and copious
report ready for iteration at five o'clock on the
twenty-seventh. Travel weariness and emotional
abrasions will be slowly and gently kneaded
into oblivion.

JOHN

The length of the letter made me feel loved. I felt even more
loved when I returned from the trek and found a second letter
waiting for me at the hotel in Kathmandu.

6 January 1984

Each day takes you higher into those rock-strewn
silences, SOPHIE, and each day's march must
reinforce your confidence in yourself for now
you are certain you can surmount any daunting
upland the future might confront you with.

No doubt the Nepalese tarai is no picnic and
therefore you'll come back prepared to withstand
vicissitudes and exigencies that lie ahead. No
more weeping unaccountably at the wheel of
your car; no more involuntary sobbing in the
night between the sheets. This excursion couldn't
have come at a better time.

At every rest/pause in the journey try to have
your feet higher than your head. Don't neglect
the minor ministrations of first-aid to blisters
and abrasions. Shun companions who smoke
and don't try to inhibit your own huffing and
puffing. Heavy breathing was the crucial lesson
you learned in your training runs. As you step
along, breathe deeply and rhythmically even
when you don't need to. Energy comes from a
steady supply of untainted oxygen. Breathe in

through your nose and out through your nose. This enables incoming air to be warmed by the heat transfer in your nostrils. Warm air gives up its oxygen more readily.

Over the month you won't pick up much of a smattering of basic Gurkhali but there must be opportunities aplenty to meditate on the grandeur of Kanchenjunga and Annapurna. Our planet is a beautiful one yet too few people can find the courage to get out there and appreciate it.

Now and then, as you pass the odd stupa, cast your thoughts back to that profligate young man, two and a half thousand years ago, who became one of history's foremost sages. Buddha had a message for you personally. He preached the ever-changing nature of your being. The trammeled mother-wife-daughter, compulsively prone to self-destruction, the person you used to be, is not the same entity who now matches her strength with the Himalaya, the land of snow. No-one can be blamed for shortcomings of the past, yet we all ought to be held accountable for misgivings about the road before us into the unknown.

Have you ever noticed how Lahsmi, wife of Visnu, resembles yourself, SOPHIE? All those delectable swellings of edible flesh and the demeanour of solemn complacency. Living so many lives concurrently, you must need all the arms and hands that can possibly be attached to you.

JOHN

It did not matter that I received his advice about trekking after the trek was all over. The content of his letter did not matter at all. What mattered was the length of the letter and the trouble he had taken to write it. I felt that I could extract, from beneath the words, the fact that he cared about me.

The next day, just before I left Nepal, I was most surprised to receive yet another letter from him.

13 January 1984

Let's hear your message for a contented world, SOPHIE. Contentment is so weakening. Is this why you are trudging sunburnt and trail-blistered across those splintered rocks and frozen scree; just to introduce a little hardship into the daily round? So far, not a word has been received from your direction. Does this mean that all your ideas and observations are going into that well-worn notebook?

At night, in that clear air, the vibrations from heavenly bodies must be an orchestration to behold. The science of astronomy began with those early Semites contemplating the starry skies over the decades. All the work had already been done, all the necessary thinking already performed, before Johannes Kepler formulated his laws of the motions of the planets.

No doubt your whole life, SOPHIE, is being symbolised by your present exertions. The reason for your success in such varied fields is obvious. You seem drawn toward the difficult and strenuous, mentally and physically. It is your destiny that sends you onward and upward. Since you believe in expressing the forces within you, it would require courage not to be courageous. Kismet.

During your absence, I have been propositioned along the following lines:

Her: Over the years we've known each other we have always got along well together.

Me: I wonder why?

Her: Well, there have only been two occasions when you behaved badly from an emotional point of view.

Me: So, because of my good record, you are going to reward me with more of your presence?

Her: I could move into your apartment with you from March the first.

Me: You only want to help me.

Her: Why not?

Me: Our lifestyles would never meld.

Her: But I could ensure that you stopped ruining your life. We only live once.

JOHN

I worried about this letter all the way back to Australia. What did it mean? Did it mean that he missed me and that, although propositioned by another woman, he was thinking only of me? And what about this woman? How could she talk of his 'emotional' behaviour when he insisted that he had no emotions? Who was this woman? What kind of a relationship did he have with her? Was he trying to tell me that, as he'd received no letter from me, he felt I mightn't care about him and he wanted me to know that he had someone else on the back burner? I had written, of course, to everyone – to him, to my children, to my mother, to friends – but none of my postcards or letters were ever received.

I came home with a terrible lung infection but I went to make love to him all the same. I was so ill and feverish that he sent me home to bed and told me to call the doctor.

31 January 1984

Those antibiotics will clear up the pulmonary infection, SOPHIE, and a few days in your familiar habitat will ensure a permanent return to equilibrium. Your Himalayan trek gave you insufficient time to acclimatise yourself and it is no surprise that the bitter air has seared your lungs. Follow doctor's instructions about the pills and get into bed as early as possible. Granted, a mother has slim chance of early bedtime; but you have to be adamant in emergencies that come along.

What you say about being intolerant of physical illness is understandable and exactly what one might expect from you. But you have to admit that you have been through extreme strenuosities recently, and some sort of reaction is not unusual.

Friday will bring you tuna, cheese and lettuce, dried sultanas, blancmange, cider. But don't feel that you are constrained to perform energetically. Convalescent conversation will be quite acceptable. If you have to be absent, try to send me word by way of explanation as soon as possible; otherwise all sorts of possibilities might occur to me.

Don't take risks. It took four thousand million years to evolve you from a single cell so don't squander wholesome health by trying to save a few days in bouncing back to your habitual zestfulness.

JOHN

I wrote back to tell him that nothing would stop me coming on Friday. I wanted him. I longed for him. I was totally and utterly addicted to sex.

1 February 1984

Sex addictive? You mean like chocolate biscuits? Should a moral conscience weigh upon your happiness, SOPHIE, you can be sure that you have the spiritual strength to quit at any time. You who have accomplished so much would find such a task easy indeed.

A slice of Dutch gouda is what will be required on Friday morning.

JOHN

I started to feel dissatisfied, irritated, even angry. In may ways John was the answer to any truly liberated woman's dream; he was a caring man, intelligent, supportive, appreciative, sexually satisfying and he didn't interfere with other aspects of my life. The truth is that Michael, my last mate, was hovering on the horizon. He had made tentative gestures which, if taken up, might well lead to a renewal of that relationship. I wasn't sure what to do. I missed the 'marriage' that I'd had with Michael. In my letters to John, I talked of my dissatisfactions, of my feelings that his refusal to go anywhere with me indicated that he was ashamed of me; of my need to do more than visit his oasis once or twice a week; of my longing to live a complete life with a man; of my wish to walk down the street holding someone's hand. I did not mention Michael.

11 February 1984

You are a fascinating companion, SOPHIE. A vigorous spirit. And you would be erring to remain contented with this state of affairs. Your successes in your several lives are due to seeking for improvement even when most people would feel happy with the status quo.

You can be quite sure that your suggestions about whatever it is that goes on between us are studied with earnest application. What you say about an aura of shame and hypocrisy is currently being decoded. As you know, procrastination and hypocrisy are my leading lights, but undoubtedly some adjustment could be made.

It is easy to agree with your contention that
your concept of friend and lover is very different
from mine. Thinking it out calmly you will have
to admit that I could never participate in your
academic activities. Nor your creative endeavours.
And certainly your knowledge of family
management would leave mine miles behind.
What you need are three or four partners, each a
champion in some field where you excel.

JOHN

I didn't want three or four partners. I wanted one man who could be everything to me. I wanted what I once had with Michael – to eat, sleep, breathe with one man. So I rang Michael up and I said, 'Why did you write me that letter weeks ago?'

'Because I missed you,' Michael replied.

'I love you, you know,' I said. 'I want you back.'

'It's a bit difficult at the moment,' said Michael. 'I've talked this lady into studying Communications in Bathurst. I might have to go and live up there.'

I cried into the telephone.

'Look,' he said, 'I've never had a happier four years than those years I spent with you. No-one ever understood me the way you did. This relationship I'm in – it's so destructive. I've got to get out of it.'

'I want you back,' I wailed. 'You're part of me.' I sobbed and sobbed into the telephone.

'I've got to go up to Bathurst for a week with her and get her settled in. We'll sort this out. Don't cry any more, love. Everything's going to be alright. I promise. I'll see you as soon as I get back.'

I went to John's apartment the following Tuesday. I knew I was going there for the last time but I didn't know how to tell him. In fact I couldn't tell him. I made love with such ferocity that my body was left trembling and shaken. It is an awesome feeling, to know that you are making love to someone for the last time.

When I got home I wrote him a letter. I told him that Michael had come back to me and that I felt I had no choice but to renew a relationship that promised to give me life-long companionship and love.

16 February 1984

No-one could live four or five years with another, SOPHIE, without becoming profoundly involved. Dreams can come true, not for everyone, but, for personalities like Michael and yourself, you know in your heart that the years already shared bode fair for the future.

What you say about grabbing things you both want and making them real has the ring of authenticity about it. Certainly you yourself have a track record of never sitting on the sidelines. You have always been in there getting bashed around and scoring goal after goal.

Life and vitality are exactly what you have to choose. You must never feel constrained to park in Royal Street again. But what you must do is remember to keep me posted on the adventurous and not-always-comfortable journey you trace through the ineffable mysteries that are popularly referred to as life.

JOHN

I wrote back, full of tears, uncertainties, fears, apprehensions.

17 February 1984

Your being full of apprehensions and emotionally unsettled is utterly understandable, SOPHIE.

But you are aware of the dangers. A family
depends upon you for stability and direction.
And the problem is not going to become smaller.
Another ten years will see you face to face with
grandchildren. The way you behave now will
influence your children's propensity to bring you
their own offspring gladly or reluctantly.

There are going to be no difficulties more
arduous than those you have already vanquished.
Your wisdom is increasing not dissipating.
You have already seen the worst that human
relationships can burden you with, and you
have made your way, not apprehensively, but
victoriously. There is nothing in your future to
bring you low.

Michael will travel to Bathurst and he will be
back in a week. Life is not going to be messy and
you are going to enjoy every second of it.

Any cuttings about your writing career would be
welcome in Royal Street.

Should you need a soothing massage, don't forget
to transmit, in advance, your estimated time of
arrival at 'Kingston'.

JOHN

Why did he have to be so nice? Why did he have to keep
saying such encouraging things to me? Why did he have to talk
about himself as 'Royal Street' and 'Kingston'? Why couldn't
he talk about himself as 'I'? And why, oh why, could I not resist
him? I wrote back immediately to tell him how nice he was
and to say that I'd come on Friday.

21 February 1984

Chicken salad is always available from the Cycle
Defrost 290, SOPHIE.

Don't spare any thought for my niceness towards
you. You can be quite sure that you yourself
are nice aplenty for several people. Don't worry
about being fretful and discontented. Contented
souls just never need to achieve anything.

You have a quiet voice and a thoughtful
demeanour. Rest assured that everyone loves to
be in your company.

JOHN

I rushed to his apartment, threw myself into his arms and
covered him with kisses. 'My stars say I'm suffering from a
passion bordering on obsession,' I declared.

'Goodness me, Sophie, we're all suffering from that.'

'What about you? In your letter you said that everyone loves
to be in my company. Does that mean you? Do you love to
be with me?'

'Oh, Sophie, I don't count. I'm not a person; I'm a robot. I
haven't got any feelings. I just tell you what I know from the
point of view of an observer.'

If only once, just once, he would say he loved me. 'You know
very well, Sophie, what pleasure you give me.' We made love
as we always did – in the same way, following the same pattern.
'You know what happiness is, don't you, Sophie? Happiness is
doing the same pleasurable things, over and over again. That's
what happiness is. Now you just lie there and I'll get you some
nice healthy food.'

We ate our lunch and chatted about Adelaide. I was due to
leave the next day for Adelaide to attend Writers' Week. I lay
in his arms after lunch and he cuddled me.

'I'm never coming back, you know, I said, stroking his chest.
'I've got to be faithful to Michael. It won't work otherwise. My
agreement with him is that he'll extricate himself completely

from that other woman while I'm away and when I get back we'll begin again. I'm not promiscuous, you know. A proper relationship has to be based on loyalty and fidelity. I'll miss Royal Street. I'll miss my oasis.'

He didn't seem perturbed. His hand reached down to touch me so that he could give me another orgasm before he sent me on my way. I had a shower after that and got dressed and sat on his lap in the armchair in the lounge-room as I always did before I left. I tried to raise my head but he wouldn't let me. He pushed my head further into the curve of his neck and held it tightly.

'I've got to go,' I said. 'I have to pick the kids up from school.' He let me go. He walked over and opened the door for me.

'Arrivederci,' he said, as I slipped out. There were tears in my eyes.

Michael took me to the airport the next morning to see me off to Adelaide. He was wearing a pink T-shirt. We had breakfast in the cafeteria before the plane took off. 'Everything will be alright,' he said. 'Don't you worry.'

There was a letter from John waiting at the hotel for me when I arrived in Adelaide.

1 March 1984

Don't expect fellow writers to be over-companionable, SOPHIE. Kurt Vonnegut talks of writers at convention groping blindly past each other like half-hibernating brown bears.

It is fairly certain that your fellow writers will have dreadful drinking habits. Be wary of them. They say if you take a job as a barman in Soho for six weeks you will not only give up alcohol, but also lose all respect for well known actors and writers and television producers and journalists as, night after night, you watch the wheels drop off them one by one.

Not only yourself, but especially your children need the presence of Michael, SOPHIE. Don't entertain any qualms about it. Foolishly he has navigated a false course but now is back on true reckoning and realises how insufferably wayward he was. Royal Street can offer you none of the effusive warmth you crave.

JOHN

I was compelled to write to him. I wrote to him every day from Adelaide. What was I doing, I wanted to know, writing like this to him when I had made the decision to give him up? Why was I so confused? Why was I so indecisive? Why was I procrastinating? If, as I had told him, I had decided to lead a faithful life with Michael, then why was I compelled to write my heart out to him day after day?

There was a letter for me when I got back home."

14 March 1984

No-one could call you inactive, indecisive, procrastinating, SOPHIE. On the contrary, you are cheerful, dominant, energetic, confident, competitive, assertive, optimistic, reckless and adventurous.

If you wish to find someone who is calm, placid, generous, affectionate, tolerant, forgiving, sympathetic and kind, you will have to call in at Royal Street. Nine-thirty on Friday morning is an excellent time to call. Your welcome is assured, your presence is desired, your personal influence becomes an inspiration well-nigh impossible to forego.

Quite properly, in the extraordinary circumstances of your present predicament you are feeling detached, ambivalent, reticent,

suspicious, cautious, awkward and reflective.
Yet the means of returning you to your normal
self are on hand. The recipe includes a hot cup
of tea, a warm massage, tepid chicken, chilled
strawberry blancmange and glacial Chopin.
Thereafter you step into the world refreshed,
eager to grapple with problems, determined
to prevail.

JOHN

How could I resist? Besides, Michael's return caused a certain amount of tension. He spent two nights a week at my house but he spoke of nothing except the lady from Bathurst. He recounted his devastating experiences of the past year; how destructive the relationship had been, how destroyed he felt, how difficult it was now because she kept demanding his return. He had mouth ulcers and swollen lymph glands. The doctor thought he might be suffering from some serious illness and Michael certainly believed he was dying of leukaemia. It was all a bit hard to take. Where was the Michael I used to know? The man who was with me was not the same as the man who had lived with me before. I thought it would take time, time to talk it all out of himself, time to get over such a destructive experience, time to heal.

I wrote compulsively to John every day, telling him how I felt, how I was coping, how Michael was behaving, and I continued my visits to Royal Street. I felt guilty about the fact that I was still accepting John's kindness, his gentleness, his passion. It was a betrayal but hadn't Michael betrayed me? I felt like a hypocrite but I knew that if I kept John as my lover, then I would be less anxious about Michael, less eager, less demanding, better able to give him time to pick up the threads and find his way back to a proper relationship with me. I became quite exhilarated, really – having two lovers.

20 March 1984

Your letters are packed with the stuff of human relationships, SOPHIE. Splendid material for any novel. Don't worry about being a hypocrite. We all are. In the best tradition of paradoxes, the only unhypocritical statement is, 'I am hypocritical'.

The Bathurst lady is known to you only through Michael's interpretation. Sometimes she is so copiously supplied with boyfriends that she has no need to yearn for companionship. Other times she is so starved of companionship that she threatens to leave her studies and gravitate to Michael. One thing is certain, she will never complete even one year of the Communications course and the reasons she will proffer by way of explanation will be forged in the latest socially acceptable fashion.

As your fifth child, Michael can live out his life span in comfort. Yet there are restrictions in the way you attend to him. For instance, you cannot discuss his symptoms with the doctor, as you could do with your own children. And Michael's interpretation of the doctor's pronouncements is probably as self-serving as his depiction of the Bathurst lady.

Mouth ulcers and swollen lymph glands? Keep an eye peeled for herpes and other sexually transmitted diseases.

Yes, indeed, your form is radiant this week. Evocative of superbly leavened, freshly-baked, wholemeal muffins. Don't eat too many chocolate biscuits now.

Next Wednesday: chicken, pineapple juice, black cherries, Chopin and much more.

JOHN

I kept to the rules. The matter of our letters was not to be discussed at our meetings. Our levels of communication were separate and distinct. Visits to Kingston in Royal Street were for lovemaking. Letters were for pouring out one's heart. My letters, that is. He maintained that he simply did not have a heart to pour out to anyone.

'Goodness me, Sophie, it must be very exhausting to be involved in all these human emotions.'

'You know what,' I said, 'I envy you. I wish I had no feelings. I wish I were calm and peaceful and restrained and detached. I wish I could be like you.'

'Oh, Sophie, believe me, I have nothing for you to envy. True, there are no upheavals in my life, but there is very little else. No, you go on just the way you're going. Yours is the right way, believe me.'

I cried a lot – while driving the car, washing up the dishes, lying in bed. And I wrote John letter after letter. Why, I wanted to know, couldn't I resist the magnet of Royal Street? Why did I have to return to him, again and again, almost against my wishes, certainly against my good judgement?

30 March 1984

The oasis becomes a magnet, SOPHIE, because of changes occurring within yourself. Relentless neural patternings. You are being conditioned to steer a measure of your life within the confines of Royal Street; just as those chunky cat's eyes along the edges of traffic lanes are conditioning you to drive within the margins of the lane. Deviate, even a little, and you are reprimanded by a rude bump against those sensitive tyres. Fail to take a smooth ride through the oasis at the appointed hour and the sudden thump of hard times gets to you with the realisation that you have strayed beyond the strawberry blancmange area.

The reason I have no telephone is because of the friendship club through which we met. One or two of the members whom I met, and three or four whom I only wrote to, had taken up the habit of phoning throughout the night. For a while I listened and sympathized, rather in the manner taught to operators at Lifeline. But in the end I asked the Telecom people to disconnect the phone. Soon it will be reconnected and you'll be informed.

Meanwhile, what you have to do is not overdo it too much. A little running is essential to keep the sparkle in your eye and the glimmer in your hair. But remember; you are not trying to improve your running, merely maintaining sound health. A little teaching is good for you, but not too much of the breathless sweating through performances for unappreciative audiences. A little family life is essential for you, but don't become weighed down with too many stray cats and lame ducks.

JOHN

I struggled on with Michael but it was not very satisfactory. I felt that he was drowning. I told him I could save him; my hand was strong enough, but he had to make the effort to reach out and grab hold of it. I didn't think he was doing that. I thought he was letting himself sink into darkness and death and despair.

I wrote to John about these matters. I didn't want John to get the phone connected. I thought that he might stop writing me letters if he could talk to me on the telephone, and I needed his letters to continue. He had become my father-analyst-friend and his letters had become essential to me.

9 April 1984

Michael will always need your guidance, SOPHIE, and you are bound to help him as you would help any soul in strife. However, in dealing with lame ducks it is instructive to remember the first lessons taught to life-savers by the royal society. The main theme is not how to bring them back alive. That is merely of secondary importance. No, the vital ability all life-savers must acquire is how to fight them off and how to approach with impunity. Michael needs you more now than ever before and you've got to play your inevitable role whole-heartedly.

Wednesday looks like a cod dish: tuna and gouda cheese, pineapple juice, strawberry blancmange, pecan nuts, bananas and pears. It seems unkind that you have to go on to work with the effulgence of your lover's manhood lying over your thighs like a baker's glaze.

JOHN

And then Michael came to me one night.

'Look,' he said, 'it's no good. This isn't working. I thought I was free of her but I'm not. I'm still involved with her in some way. It's terribly destructive and I've got to get out of it but it's as if I'm on some merry-go-round and I can't get off. Maybe I'll be destroyed and maybe I'll escape but I can't go on with you at the moment. It wouldn't be honest.'

I wasn't a bit surprised. I wasn't even angry. I certainly wasn't deeply hurt. After all, he had not brought back the Michael I loved. He had just brought some shell of himself. He had only brought the promise of happiness, not happiness itself.

I wrote to John straight away to tell him that Michael had left, that I was free to sleep a whole night with him, that I would be there on Friday evening.

18 April 1984

On Friday evening: chicken, Chopin and the
longest, slowest, most sensational massage
imaginable. Your flesh is being kneaded into the
consistency of caramel angel cake.

JOHN

How good it was to sleep beside him again, to feel him take
me sharply, suddenly, swiftly throughout the night, plunging
himself into me, time after time, as if he might, in this way, leave
an indelible stain upon my flesh.

At home the next day, I could feel him hovering across
the surface of my skin, like some mantle I wore that covered
me from head to toe, enclosing me entirely yet touching me
nowhere, maintaining at all times an infinitesimal distance from
my body. I could feel his presence everywhere, even on my nose,
my cheeks, the top of my head. How tantalising to feel him so
close to me and yet to be unable to touch him.

I wrote him a letter and told him all this and I told him that,
despite his one hundred and eight years, he did not seem old to
me. I told him I thought I had made him younger. I told him
I thought I was good for him. I told him that indulging and
exploring and expressing my sexuality with him was a great
bonus in life that I never expected to have.

24 April 1984

Observing you going through your sexual
paroxysms, SOPHIE, must be one of life's
greatest delights. The squirming pressures of
your oiled flesh, struggling to express itself. The
desperate shouts and the aroma of your sex
from your warmed body.

On Wednesday there might be an avocado.
Certainly there will be languorous hours of
massage for your shapely self.

JOHN

'There's nothing to eat today,' he says, as I walk in the door.

'I only come for the food, you know,' I reply.

'Well there's fruit and cheese and avocado. Will that do?' he asks anxiously.

'I don't need food. I need you.'

'Goodo. Very good. Oh my, Sophie, you know you walk across the room like a big cat. You're in very good shape, very good shape indeed. I don't see how anyone could ever get tired of you.'

Dissatisfaction of a kind beset me after Michael's departure. I couldn't see that the relationship with John was getting me anywhere. It existed but it did not progress. I was happy during the time I was with him. I was happy when I received his letters. But the rest of the time I was sad. I didn't want the strands of my life to be separated. I wanted them entwined.

27 April 1984

What you say about relationships, SOPHIE, is
quite correct. Relationships cannot remain static.
They have to move, change in minute and subtle
ways, develop, grow.

On the subject of subtle change are you aware
of the difference between the crystal in your
necklace and ordinary glass? There are pieces of
Egyptian glass which have not yet crystallised
after four thousand years, yet imperceptible
movement of the particles within is going on
inexorably.

To solidify, a liquid must be composed of freely
moving molecules or atoms so that these can

arrange themselves neatly into a crystal lattice. In glass, all the atoms are bonded to each other. As a result, rearrangement into a symmetric crystal array at room temperature is too slow to measure. This is offered to you in case you need a simile or metaphor in your next novel to exemplify extreme slowness.

Do you find this boring? Your being bored is a risk we take in our encounters. Goodness knows, far riskier passages of life have been traversed by both of us on our separate yet divergent careers. However, in a way of life where even the closing of the swimming season is accompanied by shock and consternation, the mere possibility of wearying you must assume alarming proportions.

In your letter you ask if I am still afraid of you. You must confess that your lifestyle is formidable. Just imagine darting from Royal Street in order to hurl yourself into teaching sessions, and thence back home to provide guidance and housekeeping in the hurly-burly of an ongoing family. All that warmth, dedication, frankness and expertise make for an overwhelming presence.

Should you have any further questions, rest assured they will be dealt with exhaustively on Saturday evening together with a cold dish of tuna and avocado, blancmange with black cherries, massage and somnolence, daybreak tea with egg and toast.

JOHN

That was another thing. I wanted to sleep at his place on Friday nights because that was the night my children stayed at their father's house and I was, therefore, free of them. However, he refused to make any regular commitment and if I suggested that a Friday night suited me better he would always say that Saturday was preferable. I spent Friday nights alone and weeping.

I broke the rules and talked about the content of our letters the next time I saw him. 'Why do you call what goes on between us "encounters"? Why won't you call it a relationship?' I demanded.

'Oh, Sophie, you're the expert on relationships. I don't know anything about relationships. Now, then, have another cup of tea.'

And he was right. He found it necessary to keep our meetings on the level of 'encounters'. He dismissed, with horror, the idea of the intricate involvement of relationships. He always had to keep himself on the edge of non-involvement so that he could make a quick getaway if necessary, so that he could avoid all those pitfalls that he watched others stumble into. He did not want to be loved because he could not permit himself to love.

I became afraid because I cannot live without loving. I thought I should exercise more restraint. I thought it was unwise to let him think I was fond of him. If he thought, for one moment, that I loved him, he would have to withdraw from me. I knew that, but I could not be like him. I could not shut my feelings away and never admit to their existence. He never thought any further ahead than the next meal or the next 'encounter'. I wanted some assurance that he would go on being my lover forever. I wanted him to share that belief. I thought that if we both believed it, then it would come true. I told him all this in my letters.

One Saturday night, while I was with him, my daughter cut her finger very badly. I wrote and told him that I would not come again on Saturday nights. If he could not sleep with me on a Friday night, then I would not spend the night with him at all.

22 May 1984

I have to leave for Canberra, SOPHIE, and will
be back in four or five days. Friday night is,
therefore, impossible.

JOHN

27 May 1984

Canberra has given me a high fever. You would
be wise, SOPHIE, to avoid risk of infection on
Wednesday.

JOHN

But I went there, unannounced. The door was locked. I
banged on the door, my heart pounding. What if he had disappeared? What if I never saw him again? I kept knocking,
knocking on his door. After a few minutes, he opened it. He
hadn't been lying. He was ill but I seduced him, despite the fever.

7 June 1984

I'm off to Melbourne on Saturday morning,
SOPHIE, so if you'd like to turn up Friday
evening you'll be expected in Royal Street.
Breakfast early, but it always is.

Don't expect a sumptuous repast on Friday night.
As you know, my winter repertoire is rather
restricted. Baked, greaseless chips with melted
cheese, Blancmange with strawberries. Plenty
of Bushell's Blue Label as black and viscous as
blood from witch's vein.

JOHN

Somehow the balance of power had changed. How had it
happened? In the beginning he wanted to know when I was
next free to visit him. Now he controlled our meetings. He

had done everything he could to win me and keep me when Michael had returned. Now that he had won, I had become a victim rather than a prize.

13 June 1984

Friday evening is impossible, SOPHIE, for my presence is required at my brother's family's place.

You will be greatly expected, as usual, on Wednesday morning next. But in the interim I shall have to let you know if an opportunity presents itself.

JOHN

I wept. I did not matter to him. I was second best. I did not come first and I longed to be first. He even put a visit to his brother's family ahead of a night spent with me. How humiliating! He was cutting me back to once a week. That's what he was doing. Wednesdays, during the day, were acceptable but if I wanted more he would, in his own way, refuse me.

Our lovemaking continued to be passionate, exquisite, ecstatic. Perhaps he was right. Perhaps this was his way of exercising restraint and ensuring that our association would last. I longed for his touch and the waiting made the actuality of lovemaking all the more precious.

'You want to put me in a compartment marked "Sophie, sex, Wednesday"', I wailed, over my avocado.

'Well, what's wrong with that?' he asked.

'I'm not an object; I'm a person,' I cried.

'Come on now, Sophie. We do very well. Very well indeed. I'll just clear away these lunch dishes and then I'll come and lie down with you and we'll have a nice nap. How about that?'

'I'm not going to write you any more letters, ever again,' I said. 'I should be writing a book and instead of that I spend all my time writing my thoughts and feelings to you. What's the good of that?'

'I love getting your letters, Sophie.'

'You don't. You're just saying that. You don't think of me at all when I'm not here.'

'Everyone likes getting letters, you know.'

'Writers shouldn't write letters. It dissipates the creative urge. I shouldn't write anything more than shopping lists. No wonder I can't write. You're robbing me of my writing.'

'Come on, now, Sophie,' he said, getting into bed with me and putting his arms around me, 'You lie there quietly and I'll tell you the story of my life.'

I wrote him another letter when I got home and another the next day. I could not stop writing him letters. He had had his telephone put on and he expected me to ring him but I refused to do so. I couldn't imagine talking to him on the telephone and he was certainly much too reserved to telephone me.

I wrote depressing letters about not being able to write, about finding life empty, about having too much to do. And I visited him regularly, every Wednesday.

3 August 1984

Much of your despondency, SOPHIE, is plain fatigue. That, and a certain amount or premonition of successes to come. Having tasted success with your writing already, you are impatient to taste some more.

Don't be anxious. Your satisfactions will come. A dearth of great expectations is pretty well synonymous with what you call depression.

Do let me know if there are any modifications
you would prefer in the way we get along
together. If ever you phone me, about six o'clock
at night is usually the time to find me at home.
See you next Wednesday at about noon.

JOHN

I wrote back immediately. How, I wanted to know, could he possibly expect me to ring him at six o'clock in the evening. Didn't he know how busy a family house was at that time?

10 August 1984

Six o'clock is a peak of compacted activity
for heads of households, as you say, SOPHIE,
particularly in Australia. Other cultures, other
lands, seem to ascribe a certain emptiness, a
mood of retreat, to the last daylight hour.

Some years ago I spent a warm and languidly
pleasant summer in a rakish red hotel on the
sterile and worn-out rocky Adriatic coast of
southern Italy. The evening meal was served
some time after nine or ten at night, so that
around six o'clock there was little to do apart
from what the locals call 'la pasegiata' which is
the evening stroll. Company was companionable,
surroundings were quaint, weather always
seemed ideal and the only overriding anxiety
was that the people I worked for would direct me
to uproot myself and travel elsewhere.

To give you an idea of how laid-back that life
was: sometimes I would have to disappear for
a few days. The hotel proprietor didn't have a
record of my name. Sometimes my bill would
have to wait for payment, yet there was no panic,
there were no recriminations, merely an air of
trust. The bill would be presented at the evening
meal when the proprietor could summon enough
energy to tot up the score over the preceding

weeks. The bill, written out in an untidy hand, would be addressed simply to: l'australiano.

The trouble with such a way of life is that any change immediately becomes hardship. Now you, SOPHIE, live under no such comparable hardship. Your way of life has the abiding merit of being splendid training for any future whereas my Italian interlude was not. This may be a blessing you have overlooked in your helter-skelter daily round.

Have no doubts about it; the admirable life is the best life. The easy life offers no lasting benefits.

JOHN

'Well, Sophie,' he said, as I lay in his arms for our after-lunch cuddle and chat, 'I might be going away quite soon.'

I was beset by panic. 'What do you mean?'

'Well I haven't worked for quite some time. Two or three years now. There's a chance of an overseas posting. They need someone with my kind of experience in Ethiopia.'

'Ethiopia!' I exclaimed.

'Dreadful place, but there we are. I need the money.'

'How long?' I asked.

'Well, they could call on me at any time, any time at all.'

'I mean how long will you be away for?'

'Oh, a couple of years, I suppose. I've always lived my life this way. You know that. That's why I have so few possessions. I need to bundle all I own into one suitcase at a moment's notice.'

'How will I live without you?' I cried.

'Oh, Sophie, you'll do perfectly well without me.'

As soon as I got home I wrote him a letter. How could he do this to me? How could he leave me? I'd grown so used to him. I needed him. I needed the oasis he provided me with. How could I live without it? And on and on and on.

17 August 1984

You will never be short of love, SOPHIE. Look back on your own personal history and you will be compelled to confess that you have never been short of anything, especially affection. Certainly, the threat is always there that supplies will run out. Yet they never have. And the risk of possible deprivation merely makes the commodity more appealing. Its value is undeniable.

The most precious thread running through all our lives is the theme of affection. Not the affection given, but the affection received. This is why we are forever looking into the eyes or our neighbours, anxious to see approval there, or at least attentiveness.

Your personal attitude to life is positive, and therefore you will always be encumbered with acquaintances seeking your affection.

JOHN

I did not believe him. I thought that no-one would ever love me. I thought that when he went away I would be alone forever.

I did an unusual thing. I invited him to come to my house for lunch the following Monday. I was astounded when he said he'd come. Although I wanted to be able to go out with him, I had grown so used to seeing him only within the walls of his own apartment that the thought of seeing him in my environment seemed quite shocking.

12 September 1984

Wiser to give Monday a miss, SOPHIE. The prospect of sudden encounters with entities sympathetic to yourself weighs upon me rather ominously. Next week is a chance for me to visit an old friend in the Blue Mountains. You'll get a missive as soon as I return and probably our next conjunction will be on Friday the 21st.

Running some mornings a week is splendid for your health, SOPHIE, and the effects are manifest. But don't forget there are plenty of sportsmen who have become crippled through overdoing it. You certainly seem to eat all the right kind of tucker. Spaghetti is just about my favourite. What people don't know about the great spaghetti sauce is that you musn't fuss with it. It's perfect just the way it comes in the can.

Arrivederci,

JOHN

I cried and wrote him another letter. Why did he have to retreat? Why did he have to withdraw from me? Why couldn't he tolerate love? Why did he profess to have no feelings?

18 September 1984

See you Friday, 10 o'clock.

JOHN

We made love but it was not as usual. He had difficulty maintaining an erection, something that had never happened before.

'What's the matter?' I asked. 'Do you find me ugly today?'

'Oh, Sophie, you're a beautiful girl.'

'Then what's wrong?' I asked.

'We can't always perform to perfection you know. We have our ups and downs.'

'I thought perhaps you didn't want me any more.' I hugged him. 'Don't leave me,' I begged, tears flowing. 'I can't live without you.'

'Now then, Sophie, how about a nice glass of Hi-Lo milk?'

I got a letter from him the next Monday.

21 September 1984

Surmise is at an end, SOPHIE. I received a
registered letter just after your departure
this afternoon. It turned out to be my travel
instructions. Qantas has a seat on this
evening's flight.

Now all that needs to be done is to pack my
belongings into a suitcase.

Never fail to maintain your enthusiasm about
life. You have plenty of what others would dearly
love to have.

JOHN

He did not say exactly where he was going. He did not say
he would write.

When I read the letter, my heart stopped still. Then it
decided to go on and it beat with erratic fury to make up for
its moment of stillness. My mouth went dry and, in my chest
and throat I felt a sharp stab of panic. It was difficult to breathe.

I folded the letter up and put it back in its envelope. I
picked up the book I was reading and began to read, as if the
moment of the letter had never existed. I read quite calmly for
five minutes. Then I picked up the letter again and took it out
of its envelope. I unfolded it carefully, as if it were an object of
extreme fragility. I read it again. I wanted to find a hint of regret.

Then I took the letter and went into my bedroom. I opened
the bottom drawer of my desk and took out the bundle of
letters he had written to me over the last year. I took them
all out of their envelopes and arranged them in chronological
order. I counted them. There were sixty-eight. I lay down on
my bed and I read the letters through. I was searching for a
touch of love.

I wanted to tear up the letters, one by one, and stuff them into the rubbish bin but I did not allow myself to give way to that desire. I put each letter back into its envelope and put the envelopes back into my bottom drawer.

I did not know what to do next. The house seemed tall and still. I looked at the kitchen clock. It was ten minutes to three. Soon the children would be home from school. I would be able to hug each of them as they came through the door.

So I waited. I didn't know how I was going to survive without my oasis. I could imagine how lonely it was going to be, wandering out there in the desert again.

WINDOW ON THE WORLD

It was Sunday morning. Eleven-thirty. Lunch-time at the nursing home. Sophie reluctantly entered the building, carefully obeying the signs that told her to press the white button to deactivate the buzzer which was intended to warn the nurses when an elderly patient strayed out of the building. She entered the lift and got out at the second floor. As always, when the lift door opened, she was assailed by the smell of urine. She turned left and made her way down the corridor to the dining room. Sophie looked for her mother at her usual table but could not see her.

'Hello,' said a friendly nurse, 'we haven't seen you for a while.'

'No,' murmured Sophie, 'I've been away.' A lie – but how could she explain to the cheerful nursing-home staff that she could not bear to see her mother more often than once every three or four weeks?

'She's over there,' said the nurse, pointing towards the windows. 'We thought she'd be more comfortable in a water chair.' Sophie's heart stopped for a moment but she was not sure whether it missed a beat through terror or joy. Over the past five years Sophie had watched the pathways to death and she knew that being transferred to a water chair was the last step. She knew that this last step need not necessarily be quick. She'd noticed people lying in water chairs for months, even years.

Sophie's mother was sitting up, quite straight, and her eyes were open. She looked very alert today. Sophie felt disappointed. She knew that, in the last stage of Alzheimer's disease, the patient curled up like a foetus. Sophie wanted her mother to have reached this stage but, obviously, she hadn't. There was a rug thrown loosely over her knees and she was using it as the object of her incessant hand movements. Her fingers were compelled to make little folds or pleats in whatever material was at hand. Sophie could see her mother's legs and wondered how such a stick-like creature could still be alive. She couldn't have weighed any more than five stone.

Sophie sat down next to her mother and took her hand. 'Hello, Mum,' she said, 'it's Sophie.' There was, of course, no response. Sophie's mother could not communicate. She could not walk, could not dress herself, could not feed herself, had no control of her bladder or bowels and Sophie could have stood up in front of her, shouted, screamed, jumped up and down and waved her arms in her mother's face without being noticed. Sophie's mother took hold of the arm that had been placed in her hands and ran her own hands up and down it. She started playing with the two silver bracelets Sophie was wearing. Sophie took this to be a human response but then her mother began picking at Sophie's flesh, trying to force it into little folds. With a sigh, Sophie took her arm away and gave her mother back the rug to pleat. Without any further attempt at communication, Sophie began to feed her mother chicken soup, mashed meat and vegetables and red jelly.

Sophie could remember how frightening it had been, those last few months when her mother had lived alone at Lindfield. The nurse who had lived in the house when Sophie's father died had agreed to stay, but Sophie's mother gradually refused to allow her to sleep in the house. She insisted that the nurse had men there at night and this affronted her sense of morality. Sometimes she would ring Sophie in the middle of the night and say, 'Well, I'm ready. When are you coming to pick me up?' There was always the worry that she would go out alone and forget how to get home or that she would turn the gas on and forget to light it. In her better moments she talked of going to Adult Education lectures at Sydney University, but Sophie and her brother and sister knew that no such thing was possible.

When her mother first went into the nursing home, Sophie visited her twice a week. Sophie never tired of telling the sisters and nurses that her mother had been chief pharmacist of a large Sydney hospital. She wanted them to know that this befuddled and confused lady had once had intelligence, power, strength.

Sophie's mother was housed in a motel-type room with her own bathroom, fridge and television. Sophie would bring her yoghurt and fruit, nuts and licorice and bottles of 4711 Ice Cologne. Each week Sophie would buy her a box of pink Kleenex tissues. She would take each tissue out of the box, fold it into small squares and place the squares one on top of the other on her bedside cabinet.

On the twice-weekly visits, Sophie would take her mother walking around the streets near the nursing home. She always had a great deal to tell Sophie on their walks but very little of it made sense. She told Sophie that her unmarried, seventy-eight-year-old sister was pregnant; that the upper floor of the nursing home was a gambling casino; that Sophie's brother kept a girlfriend in the room next door to her own.

As they walked along, Sophie's mother took endless delight in the flowers and gardens they passed, but as they made their way back to the nursing home she would become agitated and Sophie dreaded taking her back to her room. 'What is this place?' she would say. 'What am I supposed to do here? I've never been in a place like this before.' Sophie would make some feeble explanation and rush away from her mother as quickly as she could.

Very soon Sophie's mother began wandering into other people's rooms and going to their fridges and rummaging among their clothes. They had to move her to another part of the home that was full of people like her. Sometimes she would cry and say, 'What has happened to me?' Sometimes they would have to tie her into a chair at meal times to stop her wandering away. It was worse than tragic. It evoked in Sophie a hollowness that is beyond tears.

The last time they took her out was a Christmas Day. The family all went to Sophie's sister's house at Pearl Beach. Sophie's brother drove their mother up there. There were twenty-four of them, sitting around a long table, out on the verandah, just above the beach. Sophie put a home-made bread roll on her mother's plate with the turkey and salads. She didn't know what to do with it. She tried to cut it up with her knife and fork.

After lunch, they took Sophie's mother for a swim. She had always loved the water. She put on her bathing cap and took off with a slow, smooth breast stroke. She swam and swam. They were pleased that she was enjoying herself. Suddenly she started to change direction. She began to swim out to sea; swift, strong, sure. They called to her, 'Mum! Mum! Don't go out so far!' They called, her children, trying to protect her. She didn't hear them. Sophie's brother had to swim out and grab hold of her and bring her back.

Sophie could not help thinking that, if they were still a tribe, her mother would be dead by now. She would have wandered off or walked out into the desert or got lost in a blizzard or swum out to sea. Instead of that, here she was, a body in a water chair, being fed her Sunday dinner.

Sophie sometimes wondered if it would be possible to slip poison into the Sunday vegetables. She'd talked about that possibility to the children. 'Don't do it, Mum,' warned Ilana. 'They'll put you in jail. You'll ruin your whole life.' Sophie wanted her mother to die, yet it pleased her to watch her mother eating up all her Sunday dinner. So Sophie wiped the remains of the jelly from her mother's chin, kissed her on the forehead and walked out of the dining room. She couldn't wait to get back and immerse herself in the child-warmth, the chaos and the vitality of home.

Home. It was certainly easier at home than it used to be. The last five years had been less demanding, more rewarding. The kids all cooked one night a week; Mark's girlfriend did the housework and Sophie no longer spent one whole day a weekend ironing through a mountain of clothes. She'd bought five laundry baskets and lined them up along the playroom wall. She put each person's clean clothes into the labelled baskets and the kids ironed their own clothes as they needed them.

Although Sophie no longer saw the children as a burden, mothering was still exhausting. Sophie found herself involved in all the upheavals of her children's lives and it seemed that as soon as one child's problems were sorted out, another child would tumble into momentary despair.

The house was never quiet, never still. The phone rang. The doorbell rang. The children's friends would come and go. Sophie found no peace there and often longed for escape. Fortunately, after the family home at Lindfield had been sold, Sophie was able to buy a beach house, about an hour's drive from home. Here she could get away from mess and mother-hood. Here she could sit alone, gazing at the sea. The beach house was the exact antithesis to the other house. Everything in the beach house was shipshape. Everything had its place. Everything was neat. Everything harmonised. The colours were cream and beige and brown. Even the plates and cooking utensils, the sheets and towels. When the children came to the beach house they respected its uncluttered order and left it neat and tidy and clean.

Sophie's retreats to the beach house were usually of short duration because she was afraid of what would happen in the other house during her absence. When Sophie was at the beach house she liked to spend her time walking up and down the beach, allowing scenarios of the past and present to play themselves out in her mind. She would think about the children. She would think about making love. She would think about writing books. She would look at her life, assess it, come to conclusions, make decisions. Sophie liked to watch the families frolicking in the sea edge. Mummies, daddies, little children – building sandcastles and constructing catchments to trap the ebbing sea. She did not envy them. On the contrary, she felt glad that these little children were not hers, relieved that her years of that kind of parenting were over.

One day, as she walked along the beach, Sophie saw a couple making their way slowly down to the water. She thought they were lovers, playing around. They were both facing the sea and they were pressed hard against each other. They walked with the same steps, like tin soldiers with stiff legs, keeping time. The person behind was taller and held the other person tightly under the arms so that their bodies moved in perfect unison. Sophie smiled to herself, amused by their antics, not paying them too much attention.

As Sophie drew nearer she realised that this was no loving couple playing games. A mother, with her arms about her child, was guiding her severely spastic, adolescent daughter, step by painstaking step, towards the sea. Sophie did not want to embarrass them by staring so she looked away and continued walking, but not before she saw the strain on the woman's face and the dangling, useless legs of the child. Sophie looked back up on to the sand and saw that the mother had set out two folding chairs and an umbrella for shade, an esky, towels. How many trips had it taken, Sophie wondered, to get all this and her daughter down to the sea?

Sophie walked to the end of the beach and then turned back. By the time she reached the mother and daughter again, they were standing in the shallow water, feeling the waves lap around their feet. The mother held her daughter in a precious grasp, her face close to the child's ear, making cooing sounds of delight as one might make to soothe a baby who feared its first exposure to the sea. With one hand the mother wiped the spittle that dribbled down from her child's slack lips.

Sophie kept walking and shivered uneasily. What would she have done if that physically helpless child had been hers? Would she have had the courage to bring such a child down to the beach to touch and taste the sea? Sophie did not know the answer. Her only thought was that this woman's mothering would have to go on forever, whereas Sophie's mothering was showing signs of coming to an end.

Mark was going to move out of the house very shortly and live with his girlfriend. One down, thought Sophie, and three to go. Mark was twenty-three now and Sophie was relieved that everything was turning out so well for him. He had stuck to his Arts Degree and his Diploma of Education and although Sophie had found it necessary to read and summarise Middlemarch for him while he was doing English III, she knew that he had been persistent and hard-working. His great love was French but he'd been offered a good job teaching English as a Second Language and he was determined to make the best of it. What pleased her most about Mark was that he'd found a creative outlet. A few years ago he had begun to make his own clothes and, without any training, found himself able to design and make shirts and trousers, coats and cloaks, skirts and dresses. Sophie bought him a good sewing machine and felt sure that, if he hated teaching, he could always make a living with his sewing. How she wished her father had lived long enough to see this. All those centuries of Jewish tailors passing their talents on to Mark!

Although Sophie knew she would miss Mark, she was pleased that he was leaving. His girlfriend was about to begin her career as a social worker and they were obviously in love. It was time for him to move on. He had been a father to the younger children, but now that they saw themselves as adults there was considerable unhappiness for Mark in seeing that his place in the house no longer existed.

Sophie knew that the family had contributed to Mark's unhappiness by giving him a rough time over his first girlfriend. He had chosen the girl and he expected the family to support him in his choice. He was very hurt when they did not like her. She was certainly a beautiful girl and Sophie was never openly rude to her, but she did things that Sophie found intolerable. Sometimes Mark used the car to go to university. When he had the use of the car, he would pick Sophie up from work. Often the girl would be with him and Sophie would find her sitting in the front seat, as if the car belonged to her and she looked so settled there, so sure that she had the right to sit there that Sophie would find herself getting into the back seat. The girl would ring Mark up in the middle of the night to tell him how depressed she was and to insist that he come to see her immediately. Sophie would hear her car being driven out of the garage at all hours. Sophie could forgive the girl for her constant despair about life but she did not want Mark to be bound to a girl who saw herself as the helpless victim of life's cruelties.

The relationship went on for two years and Mark must have felt more and more alienated from the family as Sophie and the other children showed their disapproval of the girl. Sophie was pleased when he decided to go overseas for eight weeks, not with his girlfriend, but with another girl who had been his best friend at university. Sophie approved of his best friend and hoped that youth, sexuality and proximity might lead to a transfer of affections.

She remembered the day Mark came back from overseas. His girlfriend had come over to the house to sleep the night so that she could come to the airport to meet him. She brought bunches of roses to put in his room. She set her hair and manicured her nails. She got up at five a.m. to bathe and dress. She wore a black-and-white outfit with a tight, low-cut bodice and a wide, full skirt. She looked as if she were going to a cocktail party. She wore eye shadow and mascara and eyeliner so that her already huge black eyes started out of her skull. Sophie wanted to warn her. Sophie wanted to remind her that Mark hated make-up. She wanted to tell the girl that no-one goes out to the airport to meet an eight a.m. plane looking like that. But Sophie kept quiet.

Sophie and the other kids pulled on their jeans and old shirts and hopped into the car. 'I couldn't sleep a wink,' the girl said to Sophie, 'I was so excited about him coming home. Do you think …?' She did not finish what she wanted to say and the question she was too afraid to ask and the answer Sophie would have been too afraid to give hung between them in the car.

There were large numbers of family and friends gathered at the airport to welcome Mark and his friend. Sophie caught a glimpse of a purple shirt and a bearded face. 'There he is,' she cried.

A few moments later they emerged. Mark hugged his family first and other friends crowded around him, slapping his back, saying how good it was to have him home. The girl stood apart in her black-and-white dress, with her carefully coiffured hair and long, elegant fingernails – stood apart, waiting for him to rush into her arms. Sophie watched her. Sophie ached for her. Eventually Mark came over to her, put his arm around her shoulders and kissed her on the cheek. He looked back towards his travelling companion and saw that she was about to leave the airport with her family. He came over to her, swept her into his arms and hugged her, lifting her high up into the air. 'As for you,' he said, laughing into her eyes, 'I never want to see you again.' And then they knew. They all knew. Except for the girl. Standing apart. Her eyes wide with longing.

Mark had told Sophie that he had known, even before he went away, that the relationship would have to end. The fact that he had fallen in love with his best friend was not anything that had been planned.

Sophie could see the direction Mark's life was taking and she approved. She was sorry that he felt he had lost his father role in the family but she was sure that moving out of the house would solve the problem.

Ilana found it impossible to be polite to Mark. If he greeted her in the morning she would snap at him. Sophie tried to talk to Ilana about it but without success. 'Look, Mum,' said

Ilana. 'I hate him. Right? Sometimes that happens in families. He teased me to death when I was little and now I hate him. You'll just have to accept it.'

'But he does things for you. He's kind to you. He's good to you. He's polite to you,' argued Sophie. 'He's terribly sad about the fact that you can't be nice to him. He's your brother. Can't you be kind to him?'

'No, I can't. That's all there is to it,' said Ilana.

'If you saw this on "Neighbours" you'd cry,' said Sophie, but Ilana remained unmoved.

Ilana, at seventeen, was as unapproachable as she had ever been. She was fired by powerful passions of love and hate and these consumed her so thoroughly that Sophie found it impossible to make advances towards her armed only with logic and reason. The boys were quite different. They would always listen to Sophie. She helped them to analyse their behaviour, their reactions, their feelings. She taught them to look beneath the surface of their own actions and the actions of those around them. They would seek her advice and engage in long discussions about decisions they had to make.

Not Ilana. Sophie did not know how to be Ilana's mother. When Ilana was depressed her unhappiness was so pervasive that no-one in the house could feel comfortable. Sophie would have done anything to break the blackness of Ilana's gloom and usually managed to do so only by indulging her. She knew the boys disapproved of this and thought it unfair. They thought Sophie favoured Ilana and spoiled her. Nevertheless, Sophie continued to treat Ilana in this way because she felt helpless. She did not know what else to do. Sophie knew that Ilana would have to learn everything for herself. She knew that if she ever told Ilana what to do, Ilana would take no notice of her. And, most importantly, she felt that if she did anything to alienate Ilana, Ilana could end up hating her for life. Ilana did not confide in Sophie, but Sophie was anxious to keep open the possibility of becoming Ilana's friend at sometime in the future.

Ilana would say, 'I'm not like the boys. I don't burden you with my problems. I keep them to myself.' Ilana had a close network of friends and Sophie hoped that she was able to discuss her problems with them. Certainly people came from far and wide to confide in Ilana. She gave advice on life, love and relationships to all who came to consult her and, from the occasionally overheard comment, Sophie thought the advice seemed fairly sound.

Sophie knew that, at the moment, Ilana was unhappy with her life. At eleven, she had shown such extraordinary culinary skills that everyone had encouraged her to train as a chef. At twelve, thirteen, fourteen, fifteen, sixteen, she knew exactly what she wanted to do whereas her friends had no idea of their futures. She had it all mapped out. She would get an apprenticeship at a top restaurant, finish her training in four years and then go off to Paris where she would work and learn to become the best dessert chef in the world. It was all quite clear. Nothing would stop her.

She did her work experience at a top Sydney restaurant and, when she was offered an apprenticeship there, Sophie thought it was like winning the lottery.

The dream turned to disaster within weeks. An older apprentice hassled her mercilessly; she was required to do excessive amounts of heavy cleaning and scrubbing; she had to lift huge pots of stock on and off the stove; she was made to work many hours more than stated in the award. She was given no time to learn anything, but rushed from one task to the next. She stuck to it doggedly but came home weeping and exhausted every evening. Sophie lay awake at night, her stomach in knots.

'Anyway,' said Ilana, 'I only want to make desserts. I don't want to put my arms down into ducks and pull out their insides. There's duck's blood right up to my armpits!'

'What are we going to do?' asked Sophie, surrendering to panic.

'I'm going to stick it out for three months and then I'm going to look for a patisserie apprenticeship. I've spoken to other apprentices at Tech. None of them have to slave the way I do. A top restaurant! Who would've thought they'd treat me like this! The kids who are apprenticed at the Leagues Clubs are having a great time.'

Sophie wanted to ring up the restaurant owner and complain, but Ilana wouldn't let her. 'I'll handle it in my own way,' said Ilana. After four weeks, however, Ilana was left without choices. Her right arm began to swell from fingertip to elbow. It was so swollen and painful that it became impossible for her to work. After a week of intensive physiotherapy she went back to the restaurant but as soon as she began to cut up vegetables, the hand swelled again and became useless. There was no alternative. She had to leave.

A year later her arm was still not better and Ilana was now in a situation of having to determine what to do with her life. She had been working all year as a sales assistant and enjoyed earning and spending money, but that was not enough. She wanted to achieve, she wanted to succeed. She wanted to be famous. Ilana saw herself as a failure. She had geared herself to a career using her hands and now she had to contemplate a career using her head. The situation of a year ago had been reversed. Her friends would be finishing school and getting ready to go on to further study, whereas Ilana, having left school early, was behind them and did not know where she was going. Sophie could imagine that there would be further storms ahead for Ilana and although she would not share her anguish with Sophie, Sophie could feel it as if it were her own. If Grandpa were alive, thought Sophie, he's probably have a few tears in his eyes for Ilana.

Paul was a bit of a worry, too. Sophie thought that any mother would be concerned if her nineteen-year-old son declared that he intended to make his living as a songwriter and musician. He was attending university, in a haphazard fashion, but he'd only managed to pass three subjects in his Arts course in two years, so Sophie did not hold out any hopes of him finishing a degree.

'I didn't go to university to get a degree,' said Paul. 'I went there to learn something.' The trouble was that the Psychology and Philosophy courses made him think and the thinking made him want to write more songs and then he became so obsessed with writing the songs that he couldn't concentrate on the lectures.

Sophie conceded that Paul had no choice. He was a musician, a songwriter, a performer and that was that. What surprised Sophie was that she'd had no idea that Paul was a musician. Paul had been writing songs in his head since he was eight years old but he'd never told Sophie about it and he'd never asked to have music lessons. When Paul was fifteen the family inherited a piano and a week after Paul began piano lessons he started playing his own compositions. Sophie felt terribly guilty. She thought she might have deprived the world of a musical genius.

Piano lessons were pretty frustrating. Paul's traditional, conventional piano teacher expected him to read the music as he played for her. However, he could play a tune after hearing it once, so he had to pretend to be playing from the music, whereas he was really playing by ear.

When Paul turned sixteen, he bought a cheap guitar and taught himself to play. Now songwriting began in earnest.

'Are you angry with me, Paul, for not having had you taught music earlier?' Sophie wanted to know.

'No, no,' Paul replied. 'If I'd learned when I was a little kid I'd have been locked into conventional methods. This way I can discover and compose it my own way.'

Soon the cheap guitar seemed unsatisfactory and what Paul longed for was an electric guitar. There was a new music shop opening at Crows Nest and Paul heard that they were selling two electric guitars, for $10 each, to the first two people who were there when the shop opened the following Monday morning.

Paul told Sophie that he was going to wait outside the shop all night so that he could get one of the guitars. Sophie told him he was mad. It was mid-winter. He'd freeze to death and, anyway, things like that only happened to other people.

Paul said he was going anyway and that he was going to get one of those guitars. So Sophie hunted around for woolly gloves and scarves and a heavy coat and a knitted hat and she found an old thermos in the bottom of the kitchen cupboard. She made him chicken soup and thick sandwiches and gave him a few packets of biscuits and a bag full of fruit.

A friend of Paul's, who had a car, wanted the other guitar and the two of them set off about 4 p.m. on the Sunday afternoon. The shop was due to open at 9 a.m. the next day.

They were first to arrive and they sat in the doorway of the shop to wait for morning. It was pretty cold, sitting there. At midnight the proprietor of the shop arrived to find the two boys camped in his doorway. He invited them to come and help him set up. He said he was sorry that he couldn't allow them to stay in the shop for the rest of the night but he knew they were first and he would make sure that they got the guitars. The boy who owned the car decided to go and sleep in it and Paul stayed in the doorway.

When Sophie got back from work the next day she was amazed to see the guitar in the lounge-room. She hugged Paul and said she was glad but she still thought he was mad to even think of queuing up like that.

'But I knew I would get it,' said Paul. 'I dreamed it, weeks ago. I dreamed about the shop and the man who let us in. He looked exactly the same as in my dream. A small bloke with a thinnish face and a little pointed beard. And I even dreamed the part about him letting us into the shop. All I had to do was be there.'

Sophie did not want to believe Paul because stories like this were alien to her understanding of the universe. 'Don't be silly,' she said.

'I've dreamed other things before this that have come true.'

Sophie knew this. When Paul's cousin was diagnosed as having a brain tumour. All the family thought she was going to die. Paul was shocked by the news and he went downstairs to play the piano to calm himself. He concentrated very hard on his cousin. He put all his thoughts and all his love into her. The door to the backyard was open and suddenly a shaft of golden light bolted through the sky and momentarily blinded him.

'It's alright,' he told Sophie, 'she isn't going to die,' and he explained why he knew this to be true. He was right, of course. His cousin made a complete recovery. So now when Paul tells his mother that he's going to make it as a musician, how can she disbelieve him?

And she believes Aaron, too, when he says he's going to make it by writing and directing film scripts. Of course, his first major effort at making a feature film had an unfortunate end but that's not to say he won't make it next time. A year ago Aaron and Marcel each put $5500 of their own money into making a film. They wrote the script, hired equipment and persuaded the actors, make-up artists and cameramen to work for nothing. The trouble was that they were in too much of a hurry, didn't have enough money and, by the end of the shoot, didn't like the script any more. Nevertheless, as Aaron says, it was the best possible way to learn about making films.

'All I want is to sit in my room all day and write and have someone pay me for it,' says Aaron.

'I've wanted that since I was twenty,' Sophie replies, 'and I still haven't got it.' So Aaron works as a clerk. He likes to take casual jobs because it would be too boring to stay in the same place and work with the same people. He likes jobs that he can master quickly so that he can save his real energies for his writing.

Aaron is Sophie's closest child because he is the one who is most like herself. She tells him everything. He does not look upon Sophie as a mother. He sees her as a friend.

There is only one moment when Sophie doubted Aaron's friendship and that was on the night of his twenty-first birthday. It was a wonderful night. There was a marquee in the backyard and Paul played his guitar and sang. Aaron looked very dramatic; he was wearing make-up and a flowing black cloak that Mark had made him as a birthday present. Aaron almost made his father weep when he got up and said that he'd found communication difficult over the years but that, quite recently, he'd felt his father opening up and making it possible to be friends. Sophie glowed when Aaron announced to the gathered crowd that his mother was really his best friend. And then he did something quite shocking. With great flourish and a considerable amount of suspense, Aaron announced his engagement to the girl he had been going out with for the last six months. Sophie felt betrayed. Why hadn't he discussed it with her? Why hadn't he confided in her?

'I thought,' said Aaron afterwards, 'that it might be quite outrageous for me to do something so conventional as getting engaged.'

The following month Sophie went to the Sydney Film Festival with Aaron and Marcel. Aaron's fiancée had a ticket as well. Sophie could tell from the first screening that the engagement would not survive the Festival. Aaron and Marcel were like Siamese twins at festivals. They sat together, joked together, commented on the film techniques together, walked out of bad movies together. It did not bother Sophie, she liked being with them, but it bothered Aaron's fiancée. She was an aspiring actress and needed to be in the limelight constantly. She could not bear to watch Marcel and Aaron's single-minded devotion to the movies and to each other. She would plonk herself down between them, throw her legs over the seat in front of her, toss her blonde ponytail and talk loudly to distract them.

'Look at the way she's carrying on,' Aaron would say to Sophie. Secretly, Sophie's sympathies were with the girl. She thought Aaron was behaving abominably. She tried to explain to Aaron that any girl who has recently become engaged is entitled to feel she'll get at least some attention.

'But this is the Film Festival. It's the highlight of my year. I can't let anyone interfere with it.'

'If you feel that way,' said Sophie, 'you should never have got engaged.'

'I know,' said Aaron, 'I've made a terrible mistake. I just wanted to have the most dramatic twenty-first birthday anyone had ever seen.' Sophie was relieved when the engagement ended and Aaron resumed a saner approach to life. He should have listened to Ilana. She'd told him never, never to get involved with an actress.

On the whole, Sophie thought, she could look at the children with satisfaction. They were strong; they were sane; and their lives were leading them in directions that Sophie could not have anticipated.

Life goes on, thought Sophie. That is what John often said, lying on the bed, arms around her, passions spent. He did not say, 'Life must go on.' There was no imperative to his statement, no sense of people actively, purposefully getting on with their lives. He held the fatalistic view that no matter what people did, life would simply 'go on'. At first Sophie would smile to herself when John uttered his predictable platitude. Not any more. The idea of life going inexorably on was a philosophy that Sophie accepted totally and one from which she drew considerable comfort. It fitted snugly with her own conviction that people are what they are and therefore do what they do. You had no choice, Sophie felt, but to flow along with the tide of your own personality. If you knew all the coodinates you could plot the inevitable outcome of your life.

John. When John left for Ethiopia, Sophie did not feel the devastation that she had felt when Michael left her. She was angry at having her source of sexual satisfaction removed and she felt humiliated by her failure to manipulate John into what she would have regarded as a more normal relationship. She did several compulsive and neurotic things; she rang his telephone number day and night; she wrote him desperate, pleading letters and she drove past his flat frequently to check for signs of habitation. She did not believe he had gone. She thought he had told her he was going away to get rid of her. She thought he was sitting, motionless, hermit-like, sealed inside his flat. She wanted to force him to take note of her.

After two weeks of this absurd behaviour, Sophie stopped and became remarkably calm. She could not discuss John with anyone. The children scarcely knew of his existence and would have felt insulted because he had never wanted to meet them. She could not explain the situation to friends because they would have told her that it was such a weird relationship that she was better off without it anyway. Having made love to John for almost a year, she felt no closer to knowing him. If that were so, what would have been the point of going on? In this way Sophie consoled herself and comforted herself. It was early October. Summer would soon be here. Sophie would go jogging, do exercises, swim, spend time with the children, try to write. That's what she did and she found that her life was neither as painful nor as lonely as she had expected it to be.

One hot, mid-January day, Sophie was seized by the compulsion to ring John's number. She did not expect him to answer and was quite taken aback when she heard his voice.

'What are you doing there?' said Sophie. 'You're supposed to be away for a year.'

'I've been through the mill, Sophie,' was all he would say.

'I had to ring your number. I haven't rung it for months. I must have known you were back. You must have been sending me telepathic messages.'

'Perhaps I was,' said John.

'Can I come over?' asked Sophie.

'If you like,' was his non-committal reply.

When Sophie arrived she was hot and damp and John ran her a cool bath. 'Now you soak in this nice tepid bath for a while and you'll feel much better,' said John, in his soothing manner. 'And whatever you do, don't slip when you're getting out of the bath. We can't have any accidents here you know.'

'That's what you always say.' He turned to leave the bathroom but Sophie called him back, 'Is there anyone else? Have you got another lover?'

'Well, there is this woman who'd like to renew a relationship with me.'

'I don't believe you. Besides, I'm not finished with you,' complained Sophie. 'I haven't slept with anyone since you went away.'

'I don't think it's a good idea, Sophie.'

'Well I do. What's wrong with me? Why don't you want to make love to me?'

'Oh, I want to make love to you alright. You can be sure of that. It would be much better for you, though, if you found someone else.'

'I don't want anyone else,' said Sophie, 'I want you.'

So Sophie and John made love with such hunger and such passion that Sophie's orgasm left her weak and shaking, her limbs like jelly. 'You haven't made love to anyone else either, have you!'

'No,' said John, 'I haven't.'

'Can I come and sleep with you on Friday night?' asked Sophie.
'We'll see,' replied John.

A letter arrived the next day.

16 January 1985

There will be no Friday-night rendezvous, SOPHIE,
for the time is propitious for individuals like us
to go our divergent ways. Give me a ring now
and then for an exchange of ideas, should the
mood take you. The onslaught of my own old
age makes it unlikely that ever again shall my
emotions be so heavily involved as before.

JOHN

Old age! What was he talking about? Sophie did not know
John's exact age but his first letter to Sophie had stated that he
was in his fifties. How could he possibly regard himself as 'old'?

Sophie was furious. She rang him up. Why? Why? Why was
he treating her in this way?

'I can't talk about this on the phone, Sophie. I'll write you a
letter.' Sophie fumed her way through the day.

21 January 1985

What we both know, SOPHIE, is that you have to
have a life-long companion to live in your house
and share your existence with you. There is no
great difficulty in acquiring such a person but it
cannot be me.

Next September I'll be back in Ethiopia. And
between times, my bachelor habits make it
harder and harder to live with anyone.

Drop in next Friday evening we'll discuss your
happiness and what you have to do about it.

JOHN

Sophie dropped in and stayed the night and felt that a great contradiction existed between the way John made love to her, the way he held on to her during the night and his statement that she must apply herself to finding a new mate.

'This is not a tragedy,' Sophie,' he insisted. 'You can find a more suitable companion than me. You can do it without grief or pain. You simply must take the proper steps to ensure success.'

'How? How will I do it?'

'You've done it before, Sophie. You can do it again.'

Sophie found out that there was a Jewish organisation called Person-to-Person. So she went along and saw them. Sophie thought she might be better off, looking for a fellow Jew. They interviewed her and took her particulars and said that they didn't have many suitable men in her age range but they'd do their best and they'd contact her as soon as they had anyone for her to meet.

John was pleased but warned Sophie to immerse any candidates from Person-to-Person in boiling water for thirty minutes to guarantee utter ascepticising. Meanwhile he told Sophie that whenever she felt in need of recreation she should give him a ring and he would, of course, be very happy to see her.

Person-to-Person proved quite unsatisfactory. They only arranged one introduction for Sophie and that proved fruitless. Sophie noticed that John seemed satisfied with the idea that she was looking for someone else. Whether she actually found another man or not did not appear to concern him. He encouraged her continuing visits and she, certainly, did not want to meet any other men. She wanted John. Their encounters were always satisfying and the thought of their lovemaking sustained and supported her. She knew that he would go away again but she had the feeling that he might come back and, although he insisted that he was unsuitable for her needs, she sensed that part of him wanted to stay with her forever. He went out of his way to convince her that he was not worth knowing and yet she went on wanting to know him.

6 May 1985

It is disappearing time again, SOPHIE; this time for a rather longer period it seems. You can imagine, there are regrets and benefits in going away, yet in all probability it is nothing more than habit that urges me to accept distant postings. They have provided me with my livelihood for so long. Anything else means permanent unemployment.

Goodbye for the moment,

JOHN

This time there was no anger. No anguish, either. There was the faintest tinge of sadness. This was not an absolute rejection as his first disappearance had been. There were aspects of the letter than indicated to Sophie that she had made some head-way. There were 'regrets'; he said 'Goodbye for the moment.' That was progress, wasn't it? An acknowledgement of the possibility of a future meeting. Sophie grabbed hold of that possibility and held it tight and, armed in this way, felt ready to get on with life. She knew it would be foolish to put her faith in a man who had already abandoned her twice, so she tucked John away into a warm crevice in her mind and gave careful thought to the next course of action. These days some women were advocating celibacy as a meaningful way of life but to Sophie, a week without sex seemed a very dull week indeed so she set about finding herself a new sexual partner.

In a few months' time Sophie would be turning forty-eight. This was a fact that had to be faced. The older she got, the harder it would be to meet a suitable man. Sophie did not enjoy new sexual experiences. Novelty and variety had never interested her. She like old, congenial, warm relationships where pleasure lay in predictability and where she could feel the ease and comfort of friendship. The thought of having to find another man and then get used to him did not excite her. On the contrary, the whole idea of having to begin again seemed both awesome and exhausting.

What would she do? Sophie admired female friends and colleagues who could get dressed up on a Friday night and go out to clubs and pubs and singles bars and parties looking for eligible men. Sophie could never have done that. She couldn't even have taken the first step of dressing up. Sophie looked natural and healthy and wholesome. She did not use make-up. She had never practiced the art of attracting men by the way she looked and would have been so uncomfortable in such a role that this method of finding a mate could not be contemplated. Sophie knew that the rituals of the mating game had to be performed and followed yet she found the play-acting nature of the initial steps in the game quiet alien to her nature.

Sophie was a good listener, a good friend and a good lover. She felt confident with any man once a relationship had begun. The problem lay in finding the man in the first place. Although Sophie could not take the usual first steps, she could not sit back and wait, either. Sophie had no intention of living without a lover.

Sophie was not sure how to go about finding a new mate, but while looking through the Sunday papers, she noticed that there were a few private advertisements in the personal columns of the Telegraph. The space was mostly taken up by advertisements for questionable agencies. Sophie decided that this might be the right place to try so she paid for a well-spaced private advertisement to appear on the Saturday and Sunday of the Queen's birthday weekend in June.

A week later Sophie received fifty-one replies. Letters came from engineers, accountants, teachers, insurance brokers, journalists, country dwellers, gardeners, cleaners and the unemployed. One came from a prisoner in Long Bay goal. They were Australian, British, Scottish, Irish, Lebanese, Polish and Italian.

Sophie was overwhelmed. To be in such a position! To be given so wide a choice! Sophie imagined that most people would regard this as an undignified way to meet men. It could also be seen as a somewhat risky and dangerous path to follow, but as Sophie read over her fifty-one replies she was struck by the sincerity and loneliness of the men who wrote to her. There was nothing wrong with Sophie; she was intelligent, attractive and healthy, so she worked on the assumption that there was nothing wrong with the men either.

Sophie approached the mammoth task of dealing with these letters with vigour and enthusiasm. The first step was to create a short-list. She had neither the time nor the energy to meet fifty-one men and it was obvious from the letters than many of them would be unsuitable. Firstly she eliminated any man who admitted to smoking. She could not possibly lie in bed with a man who wanted a cigarette after he'd made love. Next she eliminated men whose letters indicated a low level of intelligence. There were quite a few of these and although removing such candidates might be regarded as an act of intellectual snobbery, Sophie knew that she would be happier with a brighter man. Tertiary education, however, was not necessary.

Over the years Sophie had found that men who had not gone to university were often more intelligent and more interesting than those who had. Achievement, success and high self-esteem were attributes she did look for and she set aside the letters of those who did not convey these qualities. Some of the letters were short and non-committal and gave no indication of the character of the writer. She removed these as well on the basis that the men who had taken so much trouble to tell her a great deal about themselves would probably be easier to talk to. She took location into account and also looked for compatibility of interests.

In this way Sophie completed the first phase of the enterprise and was left with a short-list of sixteen candidates. She knew she could not begin the second phase until she told the children what she was doing. She had to ring up and talk to sixteen men and it was impossible to do that without the children knowing what was going on. There was very little telephone privacy in Sophie's house. If the phone rang or if anyone in the house made a phone call everyone else wanted to know what was going on.

The children did not show disapproval. In fact they were very supportive and even offered to help. Would Sophie like them to go through the letters for her? Perhaps they'd do a better job of picking out a man than she would. After all, she had not been terribly successful in the past.

Sophie declined all such offers and simply asked them for their understanding and tolerance. She would need to talk privately on the telephone without anyone daring to ask her who she was talking to or what she had said. She could also need to go out two or three nights a week if she was going to meet all these men and it would be better if the children knew where she was going and whom she was going to meet.

Over the next three or four weeks Sophie went out with a great number of pleasant men. It was, at first, an exhilarating experience and very good for Sophie's ego because she was the one in control. Not one of the men suggested merely meeting for a cup of coffee. They all wanted to take her out for dinner. The men she met were kind and attentive and they all expressed the hope that she would be prepared to see them again. She told each of them that she had received a great number of replies and that she felt obliged to go on meeting the other men before making a final decision. After a while Sophie began to feel the futility of the whole enterprise. Although she was meeting theoretically suitable men, there was no spark, no magic, no real communication. Sophie began to wonder whether she could enter a relationship with any of them.

The field narrowed down to only two possibilities. One was a softly spoken Scotsman. His business life was very demanding and he was travelling constantly so that arranging a meeting took several weeks. Sophie did, however, talk to him frequently on the phone and a good rapport developed between them. She was sure he would be the one she had been looking for but when she met him the voice and the body were so ill-matched that she felt a physical repulsion.

That left a man whom she thought of as 'the old lion'. She had met him for lunch one day during the first week of this mate-searching exercise. They arranged to meet at Eric's Fish Restaurant at Crows Nest. He told Sophie that he would be standing outside the restaurant and if she didn't like the look of him she could just keep walking. He said he would carry a walking stick, for easy identification. As Sophie approached

Eric's she could see him. He was tall and upright and neat. He wore a pale blue polo-neck sweater that matched the blue of his eyes. The thick white hair and moustache looked quite elegant. He had brought a bottle of champagne with him.

Within a few minutes they were talking comfortably, as if they had known each other for years.

'I know I'm older than you expected. I didn't tell you my age in the letter or on the phone because I thought you wouldn't meet me. I'll be turning sixty-one this August. I'm an old lion, you see.'

'I'm a Leo, too,' said Sophie. 'I've never been involved with a Leo man. I've always thought a combination like that might be dangerous.'

'Twenty years ago, maybe, but I'm retired now. I don't need to be centre stage any longer. I'm happy to sit back. You'll see, two Leos will know exactly the right way to treat each other.'

Sophie was enjoying having lunch with him but she had no intention of taking him seriously. He was thirteen years older than she was and an age gap like that seemed prohibitive. He, however, assumed from the beginning that Sophie would choose him. Not for a moment did he think than any other man would have a chance.

'You go to your restaurants,' he said, 'and meet those other fellas. And when you've finished with all that, you come back to me. I know exactly what you need and I've got all the time in the world to give it to you.'

He was a retired journalist and he had written one children's book which had been published some years ago. He had planned to do some serious writing when he retired but found that it was very easy to let the days slip away.

He thought it a good omen that they were both Leos. Sophie wasn't so sure, but when she found herself in bed with the old lion for the first time she felt convinced that there had to be some truth in astrology. As soon as her stomach came in contact with his she realized a strange thing. They breathed with the same rhythm. Their heartbeats synchronized. Sophie stroked his hair and he stroked hers. Their mouths met, gently, softly, gradually pressing more firmly together. Their twin tongues touched, devoured, consumed, flaming with the same fire.

Sophie pressed herself more urgently into the curving contours of his body and felt his manhood come to life, throbbing gently against her thigh. They clung together, suffused by the selfsame glow, one body, one circle, one life. They made little noises in their throats – murmurs of pleasure, purring of cats. Lions coupling.

Sophie had serious misgivings. The stick he carried was not simply for effect. He had suffered a heart attack some years ago and the years of smoking and drinking as a working journalist had left him with a faulty vascular system. He no longer smoked but the damage caused to his body was irreparable. He carried a walking stick because when he walked his left leg frequently went numb and he needed to stop and lean on the stick until the blood circulation returned to normal. Sometimes he would get chest pains and pains in the left arm. This frightened Sophie. Perhaps he would die while making love.

'Die on the nest!' he laughed. 'There's no chance of that happening. Don't you worry, Sophie, I'm a tough old bastard and I've got a lot of living to do. I've only seen half the world and I'm determined to see the rest. Anyway, it's the men who've never had a heart attack that you have to worry about. If you've had one heart attack and survived it, you're more likely to live to a grand old age than those other blokes.'

He'd been married twice. His first wife still rang him a few times a week to complain or to get advice or to persuade him to come and change the washers in her taps. He called her 'Number 1' or 'The Dragon' and she called him 'Dad' to remind him that he was the father of their two grown-up sons. She obviously still thought of herself as his wife. His second marriage had ended disastrously. He had married a woman with children and moved into their house. The experience had crippled him and he had learned how impossible it can be to live with other people's children. He made it quite clear to Sophie that he would never want to live with her and her children, although he certainly wanted to meet her offspring.

When he came to dinner to meet the children, Sophie felt very anxious. He wore a safari suit and a cravat and looked so obviously out of place. In no way did he look like the kind of man Sophie would have chosen. During dinner he talked and talked. He did not stop. He told the children all about his experiences as a seventeen-year-old soldier in the Highlands of New Guinea during World War II. Sophie felt embarrassed. She felt angry. She wanted to jump to her feet and shout, 'Stop talking! Stop talking! Give someone else a go.' Didn't he know that he was boring everyone?

As Sophie grew to know him a little better, she realized that his incessant talking in social situations covered an overwhelming shyness. Understanding, however, did not prevent such a thing happening and Sophie often felt that the way he dominated discussions was nothing less than an act of aggression designed to assert his superiority over his helpless listeners.

'He's too old for me,' Sophie told the children.

'Don't be silly, Mum,' said Ilana. 'If he were fifty-nine instead of sixty you wouldn't think he was too old for you.'

'But he's nearly sixty-one,' Sophie complained.

The boys pointed out that he was a very friendly bloke, had a great sense of humour, loved dirty jokes, knew all about photography and had scrubbed and polished the bottom of the frypan when he washed up after dinner.

Sophie felt uncertain. He had bought a block of land up north, at Forster, and intended building a house and moving up there to live in eighteen months' time. Sophie could not imagine herself playing any role in that undertaking. However, there were many aspects to this relationship that she found pleasurable and rewarding.

When she was alone with him, she felt very comfortable. She stayed at his flat two or three nights a week and she felt as though she belonged there. She could do as she pleased in his company. He made no demands on her. She could watch television or listen to music or read books. She could make herself cups of tea and wander around as if the flat were her own.

The age difference worried her but it also pleased her. Her own sense of growing older no longer disturbed her because the face on the pillow beside her was so much older than her own. Thoughts of vulnerability and inevitable death could be forgotten because the man beside her was obviously going to die before she did. He looked older than his age and Sophie looked younger than hers, so the age discrepancy was very obvious. When they walked together in the street, Sophie thought she must look like his child. This pleased him. He wanted to be looked at with envy. He wanted other people to see that he was capable of having a woman who was so much younger than himself.

Sophie had reawakened his sexuality and for this he was extremely grateful. He was also sad to think that he had met her so late in life. If only she had known him when he was in his prime. He would have been able to make love to her a dozen times a night. Not any more. Two or three times a week. That's all he could manage. All the same, quality was what counted and he treated her body as if it were an altar to which he brought the pearls of his love.

Sophie found it strangely liberating and challenging to make love to an older man. Having brought him back to life, she felt it was her duty to keep him alive. She liked that role because it made her feel powerful. At the same time he was the father and she the helpless child who needed to be spoiled and looked after. She was his dear, precious girl and Sophie liked play-ing that role because it provided such a contrast to the adult responsibilities of her life. It was as if her own father's death had set her free to love the father, without shame, without fear, without guilt. She had not been able to keep her own father alive but she was going to do everything she could to keep this father alive forever.

Soon after Sophie met the old lion, he told her that he had been to India few years ago and had met some Tibetans who were trying to set up a Tibetin School in Pokhriabong, about thirty kilometres out of Darjeeling. He agreed to help them and he had been sending money to the school every month. He had not met the teachers or the parents and he was going to India for a month at the end of October to see what they had done with his money. The teachers wrote to him regularly. The letters were full of gratitude and respect. He was their only sponsor and for this reason they called him 'godfather'. They longed to meet him.

As the time grew near for his departure, Sophie became fearful. She was convinced that his life depended on her presence. She was sure that if he went alone he would die. She talked to the children about her fears and they told her she had better go with him. She felt some apprehension about going. She was used to spending considerable amounts of time alone and she was worried that she might find it difficult to live so intimately with another person for a whole month.

Sophie's fears were ill-founded. She felt very comfortable with him. He was solicitous and kind and she derived great pleasure from observing how deeply the Tibetans loved him. He told Sophie that he enjoyed being a large fish in a small pond and that's exactly what he was in Pokhriabong. He was a hero. He was the godfather. He must be respected and loved and waited upon. Sophie would never forget their arrival at the school in the early morning mist. As they left the taxi and made their way down to the school, the mist lifted slightly, revealing two lines of Tibetan children, each holding out white welcome scarves to place around the neck of the godfather. Sophie was with the godfather and if she belonged to him then she must be treated with equal respect. She soon found herself smothered in white scarves.

A whole family gave up their house for the godfather and Sophie to stay in. There were large cardboard signs placed on the walls saying, 'Welcome to the Godfather', and despite the poverty of the people, huge banquets of food were provided.

The Darjeeling police would only allow them to stay one night in Pokhriabong and the rest of the month was spent in Darjeeling. Tibetans from the school turned up almost every day at the hotel to pay their respects. They would sit with their godfather, chatting, smiling, sipping tea or whisky.

Sophie was not bored. Each day they would go walking through the streets of Darjeeling, visiting the bazaar, buying souvenirs and Tibetan jewellery. If he were tired Sophie would go off on her own, trekking and exploring the countryside. Often he would wake her at dawn to watch the sun rising over the mountains of Tibet and one magic night he showed her each point of the sign of Scorpio so that she could see a huge scorpion rising across the northern skies.

The high altitude nearly killed him. He had great difficulty breathing; he could not walk for more than a few minutes without stopping to catch his breath and if he lay down to rest in the afternoon he became cold and pale. Every night she got into bed with him and warmed him and encouraged him to make love to her in the sure knowledge that if he could do that he would not die.

Although Sophie got on well with him, she knew she could never live with him. She was too young, too vigorous, too strong for him. She could not live at his pace. It was possible, even beneficial, for her to slow down for a month, but she knew that she could not slow down forever. It would be like surrendering to the soft caress of death.

One night, in the hotel room in Darjeeling, when they had finished making love and he was holding her in an embrace, he said to her. 'If you ever find you need another lover, don't tell me about it. I would be most terribly hurt.'

While Sophie was in Darjeeling she had plenty of time for letter writing. She wrote frequently to the children, who were managing perfectly well without her. She wrote to other members of the family and to friends. One day she found herself writing a letter to John. It was six months since he had left for Ethiopia and Sophie had made no attempt to contact him. She thought he might be back and she thought it might surprise him to get a letter from her with a Darjeeling postmark. So she wrote to him and told him about the advertisement and the fifty-one replies; about the old lion who had taken her to India; about the mighty mountains into Tibet; about the Tibetan people she had grown to love; about the school she intended to help.

She did not expect a reply but a few days after she arrived back home, there was a letter from him in her letterbox.

3 December 1985

Fifty-one replies, SOPHIE. How did you handle them? Any information you care to give me in this matter would provide fascinating reading.

If you ever find yourself in need of a recycled masseur, do call in. Royal Street would be only too pleased to welcome you and provide you with a little healthy recreation.

JOHN

Sophie had come back from India alone. The old lion was staying another week in Darjeeling and then going to China for a week on his way home. If he had returned with her, she might never have gone back to visit John. In her letter from Darjeeling she had not at any time suggested the renewal of their association. In fact the tone of the letter was designed to convey to John that she didn't need him at all. She had a lover and, moreover, a lover who was not going to leave her at a moment's notice; a lover who did not find it necessary to separate himself from all other aspects of her life.

It was curiosity, as much as anything else, that lead Sophie back to Royal Street. What made this man tick? It was maddening being unable to penetrate the barriers of his defences.

His constant assertion that he was a robot, a washing machine, an observer detached from emotion, had always intrigued and challenged her. She wanted to break down those barriers and look at the person he had hidden behind them. She did not want to hurt him. She simply was determined to know him.

When they met, John's eagerness was greater than her own. Sophie felt secure, even powerful, because she had another lover. However, when the old lion returned from China, Sophie felt extreme guilt and decided it was not possible for her to maintain two sexual relationships at the same time. She wrote to John and explained that she had to make a choice and the choice had to be made from the point of view of being loved. When she was with John she did not feel loved.

John's reply praised Sophie for doing the right thing. Of course she should choose love. If this man loved her and she could reciprocate by loving him that's exactly what she should do. After all, love was something that John knew nothing about. Meanwhile, however, he had stocked the fridge with food: grapes, cantaloupe, mango, bananas, delicious apples and California grapefruit. Also plenty of free-range eggs, rice cakes, Hi-lo milk and canned black cherries.

Sophie resisted. She wrote and told him that he reminded her of J. Alfred Prufrock – too fearful to take the step of grasping life, missing the moment, condemning himself to a lifetime of loveless isolation.

He wrote back to say that Prufrock was right: the big advantage of living alone is that one can control one's public appearances advantageously. Only the highs are for public consumption. The lows are sulked away in closed obscurity. He added that he would probably vanish again the following September but that, in the meantime, she would always be welcome.

Sophie went on resisting. The teaching year had begun and she was very busy. She spent two nights a week at the old lion's flat and took an interest in the house he was having built. He seemed to think that his moving to the country would not damage their relationship. He intended to come down once a fortnight to visit Sophie either in Sydney or at her beach house. He expected her to spend her holidays at his country house.

Meanwhile, Sophie was becoming increasingly irritated by him. He was old in his ways and fussy and took so long getting ready to go out anywhere that Sophie wanted to scream. He was obsessed with the news and had to listen to every ABC news bulletin throughout the day. He was an old soldier in every way. Meticulous and military, he could not leave his flat without polishing his boots, spraying his hair into place and combing his moustache. He took half an hour to wash dishes that Sophie would have disposed of in five minutes. Of course Sophie's dishes would not have been as clean, but did sparkling dishes really matter?

The advantages, however, still outweighed the irritations. He would do anything in the world for Sophie and she felt secure and loved. She was not, however, disappointed about the fact that he would be moving to the country. She thought that seeing him once a fortnight might be just about right. With this realization Sophie resumed her visits to Royal Street and slipped into hypocrisy with surprising ease. Her only fear was being found out. She did not want to have to explain her behaviour to herself or to anyone else. Sometimes, if she wanted to visit John, she had to make up elaborate stories concerning her whereabouts. John was her secret lover and there was an element of excitement in maintaining that secrecy.

Not only did Sophie renew her sexual relationship with John, she also went down to the boat to visit Michael. He was living in a caravan at the boatyard.

'I've broken off with that lady at last,' he told Sophie. 'She nearly killed me, you know.' Michael told Sophie that he intended to steer clear of relationships until the boat was finished. Otherwise he'd never get it done. 'I get lonely, though,' he added. 'I haven't got any friends. You're the only friend I ever had. When the boat's finished you could come and live on it for a few months. You might be able to write there. I'm still going to build that walnut desk for you in the aft cabin.' He asked if she would like to go and see films and plays with him and she said she'd like that very much because neither of her lovers was interested in movies or the theatre. The idea of going with Michael was very appealing.

So Sophie settled into a pattern that was really quite satisfying. She spent two nights a week with the old lion, visited John once a week during the day and went to the movies most Friday nights with Michael. Sophie knew exactly what she was doing. She was having a bet on every horse in the race.

John thrived on knowing that Sophie's emotions were engaged elsewhere. The knowledge that she was not relying on him as the object of her affections somehow enabled him to become more affectionate. He did all he could to make her visits to the oasis interesting, pleasant and exciting.

The year drifted on. September came and went without John receiving another posting. He did not seem to mind. 'Life has never been better,' he would declare frequently. And Michael came and went. Despite his determination to stay away from women until the boat was finished, he entered what seemed to be short-term sexual liaisons. Whenever he did this he stopped

going to the movies with Sophie and when the sexual relationships ended he wanted her to go to the movies with him
again. At first she found his behaviour ridiculous. Why couldn't
he treat her as a platonic friend? When she thought about it,
however, Sophie knew that both for Michael and herself the
Friday night outings held an undercurrent of regret, a sadness
for the past and a hopeless realisation that the damage could
never be repaired. In the end she was glad when the Friday
nights petered out altogether.

In December the old lion moved into his new house and
Sophie went up there for a few weeks during the Christmas
holidays. She had a peaceful time and he let her do just as she
pleased. She went jogging in the mornings, walking in the
afternoons. They went swimming together. She read books and
lazily listened to music. He brought her cups of tea in bed and
waited on her as if she were a princess. She wished she could
love him as he deserved to be loved.

During the first few months of the new year he came to
Sydney once a month and stayed a few days at Sophie's house.
It was disastrous. He was an old man set in his ways and he took
over the bathroom for half an hour each morning. This created
irritating problems. She was tense the whole time he was there.
After dinner he insisted on scrubbing saucepans and frying
pans but Sophie did not appreciate his efforts. To Sophie this
was a silent criticism of her own slapdash methods. He made
jokes about walking across the lounge room being similar to
crossing a minefield. After three or four of these visits she told
him it was impossible. If he wanted to see her it would have
to be at the beach house. Even there, she was irritated. If he
were going to stay the night he would arrive about four p.m.
and he expected Sophie to sit and talk to him until they went

out for dinner. Sophie only liked to talk to people when she had something particular to say. She could not tolerate filling in the hours with conversation. She would rather be quiet or walk along the beach or read a book.

The result of all this irritation was that Sophie felt more drawn to John. They were never together long enough to be bored or irritable. John believed in having the right dosage of everything.

Sophie was expected in Forster for one week of the July holidays.

'Do you think I should go?' she asked John. She wanted him to say no. She wanted him to say he would miss her, that he would prefer her to stay in Sydney.

'Of course you must go, Sophie. You're needed up there and you know, once you're there, you will enjoy yourself.' Why wasn't he jealous? Sophie was sure that, if the situation were reversed, she would be jealous.

Sophie went to Forster for the week. Each morning, when she went jogging, she tied twenty cent coins into the corner of her handkerchief so that she could stop at a remote telephone booth to ring up John. The first morning there was no answer. She thought he might have gone out for a walk. The next morning she was sure he would be there. The telephone rang and rang. No answer. Sophie was furious. 'You bastard!' she thought. 'You've gone off with some other woman.'

Sophie's response to John's defection was to force the old lion to make love to her day and night. She wore him down to a frazzle. The Royal Street phone remained silent all week and each silence fuelled her mounting rage.

When she got back home she continued to ring John's number five or six times a day. Three or four days later, a woman answered. 'So that's it,' thought Sophie. 'He's even moved a woman into his flat!' She tried to sound calm and asked to speak to him.

'I'm afraid he's in hospital,' the woman replied. 'He's been most dreadfully ill. I'm a neighbour. I'm just collecting his mail and watering the plants. He should be home in a few days.'

She waited a week before she rang again. Surely he could have sent her a letter from the hospital, telling her what had happened. Didn't he realise that his disappearance would drive her mad?

When she rang his voice sounded weak and feeble. 'I nearly died,' he said. 'I had a burst appendix and peritonitis. Can you come? I'd love to see you.'

'I can't come until Wednesday, about eleven o'clock,' Sophie said.

'I'm terribly weak. I'll still be in bed resting. I'll leave the door unlocked so I won't have to get up.'

Sophie arrived on the Wednesday and went straight into the bedroom. He looked deathly pale and he had lost so much weight that his features were sharp and thin.

'Why didn't you contact me? I didn't know what had happened to you. I could have come to the hospital to see you.'

'When anything troubles me I have to be alone, Sophie. I didn't want anyone to visit me.'

Sophie thought she would sit down on the side of the bed and hold his hand for a while but before she could do that he said, 'Wouldn't you like to take off your clothes and come into bed with me?' Sophie thought that, under the circumstances, this was a very strange request but as he had been through such a gruelling hospital experience, perhaps he needed consolation.

Sophie took off her clothes, hopped into bed and immediately made contact with a hard, powerfully erect penis.

You can't make love,' she said. 'You'll kill yourself.' He took no notice of what she was saying and pulled her on top of him, close and tight, and as he made love to her she knew that no man had ever desired her as strongly as this man desired her at this particular moment. When they had finished making love he collapsed on the pillow, his face ashen with sweat.

'Are you alright?' cried Sophie, alarmed.

'Life goes on, Sophie. Don't you worry about me. I'm fine.'

'I'll go and make you some tea,' said Sophie, jumping out of bed. 'Some Bushell's Blue Label should make you feel better. A bit of role reversal, that's what we need.'

They drank their tea and he told her all about his burst appendix, about the local doctor's failure to diagnose his ailment. Of waking in the night and knowing that he was going to die, of pulling on his overcoat and going downstairs to hail a cab, of speeding to Royal North Shore Hospital, of being operated on immediately, of being told that if he'd left it for another hour he would certainly have died.

'I can't stay too long,' said Sophie. 'I have to go to work.'

John grabbed hold of her. 'When are you coming back?'

'I don't think sex is a good idea when you're all stitched up like that,' Sophie replied.

'Sex is essential. Absolutely essential.'

'I'll come on Friday afternoon, then,' agreed Sophie.

The post-hospital John was different from the pre-hospital John. Having always considered himself invulnerable, John had now touched death and the experience had frightened him. The man who had been able to run in the City to Surf race quite easily now had difficulty walking the few steps to the bathroom. He found it difficult to believe that such a thing could have happened to him and he was determined to recover his physical strength as quickly as possible. He wanted Sophie to visit him as often as she could, using his capacity for love-making as the indicator of his well-being. If he could make love, there couldn't be too much wrong with him.

Sophie rang John every day and usually saw him twice a week. Whenever she rang he wanted a complete daily bulletin of what Sophie had been doing. He also wanted to know exactly what each of Sophie's children had done, thought and felt every day. Sophie wondered what had prompted this change. Had the brush with death allowed John to drop some of his defences? It seemed to Sophie that he now accepted his need to be nourished by her warmth, her vitality. Even though he could not involve himself in the other strands of her life he wanted to know every detail of every aspect of her life so that he could, in some way, become a part of it all. Sophie could see clearly what was happening. John was beginning to live her life vicariously.

He had become softer, gentler, kinder. When he recovered his strength he surprised Sophie by suggesting that they should go to a movie. He thought it would be a good idea to see Crocodile Dundee at the theatre at Warringah Mall. He did not offer to drive her there but said he would meet her outside the box office. Sophie felt slightly nervous about going because she had never been with him in the outside world. She felt calm, however, when she saw him standing there because he looked so nervous and uncomfortable that her own anxieties seemed insignificant. She held his hand, all through the movie, and hoped he found some comfort in that.

Having gone to the movies once, he was prepared to go again and she felt he was doing this in order to please her. One day, after she had showered and washed her hair she told him she was sorry but she'd had to use two towels, one to dry her body and one for her hair. When she arrived the next time he had bought two large bath towels. It was months before she realized that he never used the new towels himself. They were just for her. The more he did to show he cared for her the more she came to care for him, and yet she remained wary about displaying emotion, fearful that if he thought she loved him he might easily run away.

'You don't come often enough,' he complained. 'I'm sure you could find time to call in for a cup of tea.'

A few months after the appendix operation it became obvious that John's stomach had not been properly sewn back together. A bulge appeared and the bulge grew larger and larger. Although the surgeon had saved his life, John had been left with an unsightly stomach. He would have to go back for a second operation some time in November.

John told Sophie that the doctor could not give him a definite date. It was a matter of availability of beds. He was not sure which hospital he would be going to, either the Mater or Royal North Shore. In any case he would only be in hospital for a week and he made her promise not to visit him.

When there was no answer to the Royal Street phone Sophie decided to ring the hospitals to see how he was. She rang both but neither had him registered as a patient. Again she felt angry. He'd run off and left her and was too afraid to tell her. He must have decided that he was allowing himself to get too close to her. He needed to do his usual disappearing act in order to avoid emotional entanglement.

A week later he answered the phone, said he was well and hoped to see her as soon as possible. When she arrived he was sitting in his armchair looking quite healthy. She sat down on his lap, as she usually did when she arrived.

'Which hospital did you go to?' Sophie asked.

'The Mater,' replied John.

'Okay,' said Sophie, 'now I want a quick answer to this question. If you were a patient in the Mater Hospital, how come they didn't have your name on their lists? You've got five seconds to think up a really good answer.'

'Well,' he said, rubbing his hand over his eyebrows and looking to the floor, 'there were these books, you see, these books I wrote years ago. I thought you might recognize the name so I used another one. John is my middle name and I made up the other one. I thought that if you knew I'd had books published, that might influence the way you saw me.'

'What books? When?' Sophie wanted to know.

'It's all so long ago. Sophie. It really doesn't matter any more. They were published in England. Three of them. The first two were reprinted as Penguin paperbacks. I won a prestigious award with the second one.'

'You mean you're a successful writer and you never told me!' Sophie was so shocked that she was shaking.

'I'm not a successful writer, Sophie. I was in London between contracts. I had to earn some money while I was waiting for my next United Nations posting so I thought I'd write a book. I only did it for the money. I found out pretty quickly that there was no real money in writing books so I stopped. I thought it was all a bit of a joke, really.'

Sophie had to laugh. She thought it was the greatest joke of all time. And he was right. If she had known this when she first met him it would have coloured her view of him.

'And you see, once I'd given you the false name, I couldn't go back on it. I had to keep the lie going.'

'It must have been a bit difficult for you, to keep up this pretence,' said Sophie.

'Not really, Sophie, and I've known, lately, that it was only a matter of time before you caught me out. In fact, I rather thought you suspected something of the kind.'

'Never. Never,' insisted Sophie. 'You fooled me completely. But if you'd written books and they were successful, how could you possibly have stopped writing?'

'That's the difference between you and me, Sophie. You're a real writer. You're compelled to do it. It meant nothing to me once I realized I couldn't make a living at it.'

Sophie immediately wanted to read the books but he hadn't even bothered to keep copies for himself. He said that she would find them in a few university libraries.

There was more shock to come. When Sophie borrowed the books from the library, she learned his date of birth and the fact that he had been a P.O.W. in World War II. This knowledge was almost impossible for Sophie to accommodate. John was ten years older than she thought him to be. Ten years! She read the books greedily, hoping to learn more about him from what he had written, but not surprisingly, John was a writer who put very little of his inner self into his books. The books were extremely well written, clever and absorbing, but they stayed well and truly on the surface level of consciousness. No soul-searching or depth of analysis here.

'Why did you lie about your age?' she demanded the next time she saw him.

'I had to. Your advertisement said you were looking for someone in their forties. I thought the fifties sounded reasonable but I didn't think you would give any time to someone in his sixties.'

'I suppose you're right,' agreed Sophie. Sophie did not mind John being older than she thought he was because he had always seemed ageless to her. The knowledge did, however, make a difference. It made him appear more vulnerable, and therefore more precious.

Now he told her more and more; his love of the army; his excellence in drawing maps; his capture at Tobruk; his years in prison camps; his belief that he had been sterilized by the Germans; his escape from the camp on his twenty-first birthday with a bullet in his shoulder; his journey through occupied Europe; crossing the Alps to freedom in Switzerland. He told Sophie stories all the time; stories of childhood, of adventure, of life in Africa. Sophie listened to them all, hoping to glean from them some understanding of what had gone into creating his character. And yet he remained an enigma. He did not tell any story from the viewpoint of trauma. On the contrary, every story was told as being part of life's great and wonderful adventure. He would say to Sophie, 'I'm fragile, you know. I'm a hothouse flower,' and Sophie knew that this was true but she did not know exactly which events in life had caused him to withdraw. She wished she could be inside his head for just five minutes. If only she could do that she might be able to understand everything.

'I don't count,' Sophie,' he would say. 'I've always drifted along letting life take me where it will.' Sophie believed him and she could see that, post-hospital, he had succumbed and allowed himself to flow with Sophie and see where that would lead him. Was that the clue to his nature? He did not act; he did not initiate anything; he only responded to what was there. Whatever the truth was, Sophie now felt secure. She had lost the fear that he would leave her and although he claimed that he knew nothing about love, nevertheless now, when she was with him, she felt loved. The closer she grew to John the more impossible it became to maintain the other relationship. She made excuses to the old lion and hardly ever saw him, knowing she would have to find the courage to tell him that it was over.

The following year John was beset by further physical difficulties. The specialist had still not fixed his stomach and the telltale bulge began to emerge again. He was forced to go to a different hospital and undergo another operation before his stomach was properly sewn up. He needed to have a small eye operation and, as he would be unable to drive for two or three weeks, he asked Sophie to mind his car for him. He would tell her when he wanted it back. It was not a new car but it was beautifully kept. It was low and sporty and solid.

'That car suits you very well, Sophie, don't you think? It looks as if it were made for you. I think you'd better keep it.'

'You can't give me a car,' Sophie declared.

'I don't really need it and you've got three boys driving your car as well as yourself. I can't imagine anyone in the world who needs a second car more than you do. We'd better go down to the motor registry and get them to fix up the paperwork.'

It happened to be Sophie's birthday but she did not think that had anything to do with it. John did not believe in either giving or receiving birthday presents. Sophie did not see the car as a gift of love. That would have been foolish. She was sure that he had given her the car simply because she needed it.

At the end of each visit to Royal Street, John would fare-well Sophie in exactly the same way. 'Now then,' he would say, 'drive carefully and don't forget to ring me in the morning and tell me absolutely everything. You're my window on the world, you know.'

Sophie telephoned John at about seven-thirty each morning. She told him all that had happened to herself and to the children on the previous day. He encouraged Sophie, telling her every day how well she was dealing with her life. How lucky she was, Sophie thought, that her need to tell him everything corresponded to his need to listen to everything.

Sophie had stopped believing in forever. She knew that everything had its time and place. Nevertheless, she wanted John to be her friend and lover forever. They had managed to create for themselves a world that was separate, satisfying and self-sufficient. Sophie knew that she would cling to that world, cling to it and hold onto it for as long as she possibly could.

Also available from Leone Sperling

WHAT ABOUT LOVE?

PART 1
NAOMI AND BETH (1950)

Naomi got off the school bus at the bottom of Hardy Street and began the long walk home up the hill. She could have stayed on the bus for another fifteen minutes while it meandered through North Bondi and along up into Dover Heights. If she had done that she could have got off the bus at the top of her own street, Kippara Road. From there it was only a short walk home. Cross the road, go past the Goldman's house, turn in at the Cohen's and take the short cut through their place, along the back of their house, down a side path and up a few steps into her own backyard.

Instead here she was, trudging up Hardy Street, lugging her heavy, first-year-high-school Globite suitcase, the handle cutting into her palm, her fingers going white and numb.

Every so often Naomi changed hands but the suitcase seemed to get heavier and heavier. She sweated under her Panama school hat. The brown lisle stockings they all had to wear to school, every day, summer included, felt wet and clammy behind her knees. Half-way up the hill, with the worst part still to come, she put her suitcase down, fumbled under her brown tunic, undid her suspenders and rolled her stockings down around her ankles. Then she took off her hat and held it, by its thin elastic, over her free arm and set off again up the hill.

The truth of the matter was that she did not want to arrive home. That's why she had chosen the difficult way of getting there, as if walking up the hill would give her time, prolong the moment, perhaps even prevent her getting home at all. If she had taken the easy way and stayed on the bus, she might have run into the Goldmans or the Cohens. The Goldmans did not have any children but they did have a black and grey Cocker Spaniel. They treated him as if he were their child. He had bulging, mournful eyes, surprisingly like Mrs Goldman's. At this time in the afternoon Mrs Goldman was often on the front lawn playing with her dog, throwing a ball for the dog to fetch and cuddling his big ears and kissing his wet nose every time he brought it back to her. If she had seen Naomi walking down from the bus she would surely have asked about Mother, in solemn tones, and Naomi would have felt uncomfortable. She would not have known what to say.

And if the Cohens had been home, that would have been even worse. What if Naomi had walked past their kitchen window and seen big grown-up seventeen-year-old Valerie in there, cooking her after-school potato chips, or little bent over Granny Bessy, who had once had her photograph taken sitting on a camel in front of the Pyramids in Cairo, or flushed Auntie Vicky (who was not a real Auntie but behaved like one) with an afternoon glaze in her pale blue, rheumy eyes. They would have made Naomi come inside. There would have been an interrogation, an inquisition. Better to trudge up the hill and avoid possible confrontations.

Naomi knew every step of the hill. She had walked home this way every day from primary school. But when you went to primary school you had a light leather satchel you wore on your back. It was easy then. And besides, there was her little sister Beth accompanying her. Chatting, laughing, playing games on the way home. Naomi looked to the left. Soon she would be at the top of the hill, level with Dover Heights School. She eyed the school with disdain. 'Dover Heights Domestic Science High School' - that's what the sign said. A school for girls who were only clever enough to learn cooking and sewing. Not the right place for Naomi who went to Sydney Girls' High at Moore Park and learned Science and Mathematics, English and History, French and Latin. She was top in Science and History. She was going to be a doctor, like Daddy. Or perhaps a lawyer.

Naomi reached the top of the hill and turned into Kippara Road. She had to cross over to the left hand side of the road because the house on the right hand side had a frightening black and tan kelpie dog that barked furiously when anyone walked by. She walked quickly up the short hill and across the road to her house. It was a large, tall, double-storeyed, red-brick house with a garage underneath and spacious windows right across the front of both levels of the house. Naomi had to walk around to the back because she did not have a front door key. Mother was always home. The back door was always unlocked.

There were two back doors to the house. The first was the laundry door but Naomi ignored that one, walked past the kitchen window and opened the door that led straight into a room they called the breakfast room.

'Mother,' she called. 'Mother, I'm home.' She looked through the servery into the kitchen but the kitchen was quite dark and empty. The kitchen steps were out next to the bench beside the stove. The cupboard above the stove was ajar and a round biscuit tin was sitting, open, on the bench. An empty glass, whitened with a film of milk, stood beside the biscuit tin. That meant Beth was home from school and had helped herself to afternoon tea. 'Beth,' she called. No answer. Probably up in her bedroom, playing with her dolls. Naomi walked through the breakfast room to the bottom of the stairs. The glass slid-ing-doors to the lounge-room were open and she could see her mother sitting at one end of the lounge, turned sideways, as if she were talking to someone else seated at the other end.

She was elegantly dressed and one high-heeled, stockinged leg was crossed over the other, her skirt drawn up to reveal her knees. One elbow lay gently on the back of the lounge and the other rested on her crossed knee, balanced in such a way that her forearm reached towards her face, her hand free to softly stroke her elongated neck. Her short, sleek, dark hair enhanced the perfect profile. The Venetian blinds were closed, the curtains drawn.

Naomi left her suitcase and hat at the bottom of the stairs and went into the lounge-room. 'Mother. Mother, it's me, Naomi. I've just got home from school.' Naomi spoke the words in what she thought to be a natural, conversational manner. She spoke the words gently, lovingly, hopefully. Mother did not reply. Mother did not move. Mother sat, stroking her neck, staring at nothing. Like a picture Naomi had once seen in a book on Ancient Egypt – yes, that's what Mother looked like. She looked exactly like Nefertiti.

Mother had been acting strangely for two months now. Since her birthday, early in October. Daddy had taken them to Tattersall's Club in Elizabeth Street as a special treat for Mother's fortieth birthday. Each birthday in the family was celebrated in this way. Naomi and Beth always had fruit cocktail for an entree and then mixed grill with chips and peas. Daddy always had ox-tail soup and well done fillet steak with green beans and mashed potatoes. Mother always had half a dozen oysters followed by grilled lobster. Jews were not supposed to eat such things but Daddy let her eat them on these special occasions. He would never have allowed prawns or lobster into his house, or bacon or pork or ham. Naomi could not imagine eating oysters. They looked absolutely revolting. She shuddered when she watched Mother letting them slide down her throat, unchewed. The really, really special thing about eating dinner at Tattersall's Club was the Bombe Alaska Daddy would order for their dessert. It came to the table with a blue flame of alcohol burning a brown crust over its dome-like top. There was fruit salad inside under the yummy soft marshmallowy mound and hard meringue at the bottom. It was ecstasy. It was a Saturday night, that night of Mother's fortieth birthday and there was a band playing dance music – waltzes and tangos and sambas. Naomi hoped Daddy would dance with Mother because Mother looked so elegant. Her dress was soft chiffon in blues and purples and she had smart black patent leather high-heeled shoes. Looking at Mother made Naomi feel like an elephant. Although she was only thirteen, Naomi's breasts were at least twice the size of Mother's and Naomi's hips swelled out below her waist while Mother's slim, boyish build seemed to have no curves at all. Beth would be like Mother. Beth was eleven and thin as a whippet.

'Is my precious girl going to dance with me?' said Daddy. Naomi kept her eyes down and took another spoonful of Bombe Alaska. She felt a clutch of panic in her chest and the food would not go down. She coughed and spluttered, choking on her mouthful, causing flushes of heat to flare from her chest to her throat, over her chin and lips, burning bright red in her cheeks. She grabbed her orangeade and gulped greedily. 'You know I hate dancing, Daddy. Dance with Mother. It's her birthday.' She took another helping of dessert and did not dare to look up until she could sense, by the scraping of chairs and slight movement of the table, that Daddy and Mother were safely on the dance floor.

WHAT ABOUT LOVE?
is available for Kindle, iBooks and POD at

www.cilentopublishing.com

AUTHOR'S BIOGRAPHY

Leone Sperling was born in Sydney in 1937, attended Sydney Girls' High School and graduated from Sydney University with a BA Honours degree in English literature. She taught English full-time with the NSW Department of TAFE for twenty years, a career that she found rewarding and fulfilling. She regards the fact that she did find time to write as a minor miracle because her marriage ended when her children were very young.

Three books, Coins for the Ferryman, Mother's Day and Oasis were published between 1981 and 1990. She was awarded a Literature Board grant in 1985. She has also had several short stories and articles published in national newspapers and Australian anthologies. These are now collected in The Book of Life.

After taking early retirement she wrote two novels, What About Love? and Jamie. She then undertook a four-year naturopathic Diploma in Nutrition. Leone now enjoys close, mutually rewarding relationships with her four children and six grandchildren and studies Latin with Continuing Education at Sydney University. Severe hearing impairment has resulted in the need for a Cochlear implant. For several years Leone has been on the Management Committee of Better Hearing Australia's Sydney branch and spends a considerable amount of time as a research volunteer with Cochlear and with the National Acoustic Laboratories.

Leone's writing is open and honest. Her style is spare and simple but constantly displays a willingness to confront and examine both the joyful and the darker aspects of human emotions and relationships.